THE **SHERLOCK HOLMES/ LUCY JAMES** MYSTERIES

THE LOCH NESS HORROR

THE SHERLOCK HOLMES AND LUCY JAMES MYSTERIES

The Last Moriarty
The Wilhelm Conspiracy
Remember, Remember
The Crown Jewel Mystery
The Jubilee Problem
Death at the Diogenes Club
The Return of the Ripper
Die Again, Mr. Holmes
Watson on the Orient Express
Galahad's Castle
The Loch Ness Horror

THE SHERLOCK AND LUCY SHORT STORIES AND NOVELLAS

Flynn's Christmas
The Clown on the High Wire
The Cobra in the Monkey Cage
A Fancy-Dress Death
The Sons of Helios
The Vanishing Medium
Christmas at Baskerville Hall
Kidnapped at the Tower
Five Pink Ladies
The Solitary Witness
The Body in the Bookseller's
The Curse of Cleopatra's Needle
The Coded Blue Envelope
Christmas on the Nile
The Missing Mariner
Powder Island
Murder at the Royal Observatory
The Bloomsbury Guru
Holmes Takes a Holiday
Holmes Picks a Winner

Sign up for our mailing list at SherlockAndLucy.com
and get a FREE download of four adventures and audiobooks

THE **SHERLOCK HOLMES/
LUCY JAMES** MYSTERIES

THE LOCH NESS HORROR

BY **ANNA ELLIOTT**
AND **CHARLES VELEY**

This is a work of fiction. Names, characters, organizations, places, events, and incidents are either products of the author's imagination or are used fictitiously.

Text copyright © 2022 by Charles Veley and Anna Elliott
All rights reserved

No part of this book may be reproduced, or stored in a retrieval system, or transmitted in any form or by any means, electronic, mechanical, photocopying, recording, or otherwise, without express written permission of the author.

Typesetting by FormattingExperts.com
Cover design by Todd A. Johnson

Prologue: Violet

"Still poking that long nose where it doesn't belong, aren't ye, Leverton?"

The man's voice penetrated the fog of Violet's unconsciousness. Smirking, insinuating, and somehow ... familiar?

The words carried her back through the years. Jagged shards of memory stabbed her.

Schoolyard taunts from the other children. Haggy. Little witch.

Her father, lying dead on the floor of yet another saloon bar after Violet had failed—again—to persuade him to come home.

Her mother, white-faced with terror, hissing at her to run, to fetch the police, while the front door of their apartment shuddered under the force of Cassidy's blows.

'Brick' Cassidy—the man who had killed her father in a barroom brawl and then run away—was a drunk with a nasty temper and a subnormal intelligence. But even he was smart enough to realise that he couldn't be prosecuted if the witnesses to his crime were dead.

Violet had tried. She'd run, sick with fear, to the nearest police station and half begged, half dragged the officer on duty to come. But she'd been too late.

After, she'd watched the man who'd killed both her father and her mother being led away in handcuffs, cursing and swearing he'd get even with her when he got out of prison …

No. Violet slammed the door on those memories. No.

Whatever fresh nightmare was in store for her now, she'd at least left that life behind.

The cloying, sickly sweet smell of chloroform clogged her nose and throat, and whatever surface she lay on rattled and bounced, tossing her painfully from side to side.

A carriage.

It was only a small piece of certainty, but she clung to it all the same. She was in a carriage. Lying on the floor of a carriage with at least one man who thought she was more deeply unconscious than she really was.

Her muscles were refusing to obey her, and she couldn't even force her eyes to open, so it was hard to see how she could leverage that small certainty to any advantage. But maybe if she could straighten her tangled thoughts, think clearly …

Memories returned, no longer knife sharp, but hazy, like stray wisps of cloud.

Walking along a busy London street. A huge black carriage, driven too fast, bearing down on her.

Hands seizing her, a pad pressed over her nose and mouth.

Even in the foggy haze that currently shrouded her, Violet's heart pounded in remembered panic.

This wasn't helping. She took a breath and tried to think.

Another memory-wisp floated across her mind's eye: an image of a boy and a girl, both with blond hair.

The children who worked for Mr. Holmes.

Becky and Flynn.

Yes, that was right. She'd been on her way … on her way somewhere, with something pressing, something terribly important to do.

The exact mission she'd been on slipped and slithered away from her when she tried to grasp at it. But the pulse-racing sense of urgency remained.

She'd spotted the children, who had been shadowing her.

She'd told them they could keep following her at a distance. Which meant that unless Becky and Flynn had been captured, too, there were at least two people in the world who knew what had happened to her.

The man's voice spoke again, and this time it was accompanied by a hard jab in Violet's ribs. He'd prodded her with the toe of his boot.

"Still pryin' into matters that are no concern of yours."

The voice was rough with a thick Scottish brogue. She knew whoever was speaking to her. If only she could claw her way back to consciousness—

Urquhart.

The name—just the name—surfaced from the depths of Violet's memory first.

Then a man's face: sharp-featured, lean, with a sneering smile and hollow cheekbones.

Violet had to clench her teeth to keep from gasping. This time, it wasn't a stray wisp of memory that returned, but a solid chunk that hit her like another kick in the ribs.

Owen Urquhart, chemist and right-hand man to Benjamin Blinder, who had stolen one million dollars in bearer bonds from the United States government.

Violet had been trying to get the bonds back. She'd known—or thought she'd known—where they were to be found.

But she hadn't told Sherlock Holmes or anyone else, hadn't wanted to involve anyone else in her mission.

Hadn't wanted to share the credit for the find, a voice at the back of her mind sneered.

Well, what if she hadn't? Recovering the bonds could have got her job back. She'd have been an agent of Pinkerton's Detective Agency again, instead of being forced to take whatever freelance work—mostly sordid divorce cases—she could find.

But she'd gone racing off without a contingency plan, without any backup except for the two children.

A different voice spoke in her ear, although this time it was only another fragment of memory, and a particularly sharp-edged one at that.

Preston, looking at her from under half-lidded eyes, and drawling, *Try not to be stupid, Leverton. You just might live longer.*

Violet gritted her teeth so hard that her jaw ached. She had to survive this. Wherever Urquhart was taking her, whatever tortures he had planned, she was going to live through them, find a way to escape—and what was more, see Urquhart and Blinder both locked up behind bars.

Because she was not going to allow her last act here on earth to be so stupid that it presented Preston with a magnificent opportunity to say, *I told you so.*

Chapter 1: Watson

London, July 1900

The case of the Loch Ness Horror began as Holmes and I were travelling home from Galahad's Castle. Holmes was in one of his ill-tempered moods. He barely spoke as we rode the train back to London. The day was a hot one. The air inside our cab from Victoria Station felt stifling, and traffic moved slowly. It took us nearly a half hour to reach Whitehall, normally a five-minute journey.

Then our cab stopped.

"At this rate, we won't reach Baker Street for another hour," I said.

Holmes said nothing.

I lifted my window and leaned out to survey the melee of horse-drawn carts and omnibuses and lorries and cabs. Loud and irate protests of drivers and passengers filled the air.

"For a Sunday, the streets are unusually crowded," I said.

Holmes said nothing.

"But only in our direction. Traffic coming our way on the other side is flowing freely. I don't see the cause of the delay."

I closed the window, which at least blocked the dust and shut out some of the noise.

Holmes said nothing.

I tried again to engage him in conversation, this time taking a more direct approach.

"Why so glum?" I asked.

"I am preoccupied, Watson," he said.

"Why?"

"Because we failed."

I knew he was referring to the Galahad's Castle case.

"'Failed' is a bit harsh, surely," I replied.

"It is accurate." He folded his arms across his chest.

"Not entirely. Two murderers are now imprisoned in Tottenham, thanks to you. That is a success, and a significant one at that."

He shook his head. "I delayed when I ought to have acted."

"When?"

"This morning I allowed Miss Leverton to pursue a plan she had devised. Out of respect and deference to her abilities, I did not even ask her what her plan was. I simply said I would wait for her to act. I ought to have demanded that she work with me."

"Why?"

"I had deduced what she would do. And if I could do that, others could do so as well, and get there first."

"Get where?"

"To the stolen bonds we had first set out to recover. As you will recall, they are worth one million dollars. Mr. Brown's criminal colleagues have been searching for them ever since Mr. Brown brought them to England. If they have been following him, or following Miss Leverton, it is all too likely that they will have hit upon the correct solution. Even now, they may have another million dollars to employ for their evil purposes."

"I think you ought to acknowledge your success," I said.

Holmes rapped on the cabman's panel. "Driver, turn around. Take another route," he said.

He folded his arms again and refused to be drawn into further discussion until, after what seemed hours but was really more like forty minutes, we finally reached home and mounted the steps to our sitting room.

I had earlier entertained the hope of a cold drink and a relaxing hour on our sofa, followed by a leisurely supper at one of our favourite restaurants. But after hearing Holmes's regrets about his previous delay, I expected him to take immediate action.

Then Holmes opened our hallway door, and I realised our path would have to go in a different direction.

Mycroft Holmes awaited us.

CHAPTER 2: VIOLET

Violet had tried to stay awake, but she was drifting through foggy darkness once again, with scraps of memory appearing and disappearing in her mind's eye in time to the jouncing of the carriage and the steady *clop-clop* of the horses' hooves.

The Silverman's patent medicine factory, where all of this had begun. She could see it now: a huge, looming brick building outlined against a grey winter sky, with smoke stacks jutting up like broken teeth.

The factory workers had started falling ill. Poisoned, the police suspected. But they couldn't prove it. No one could prove it.

The kaleidoscope in Violet's mind shifted, this time to an image of a fat, oily-looking man with a nose that had been broken and improperly set.

Benjamin Blinder, owner of Blinder Patent Medicines, Silverman's main competition.

Blinder had sat in Mr. Pinkerton's office, asking to hire one of his detectives for protection against whatever had happened at the Silverman's plant.

Blinder gestured decisively with the cigar he'd been puffing on. "If someone's targeting factory workers, Mr. Pinkerton, I want to be sure that my people are well protected."

He'd probably had no idea how phony his expression of earnest concern had looked on his course-cut features.

If Mr. Pinkerton had noticed, he hadn't cared. Mr. Pinkerton Junior, who ran the detective agency now, wasn't at all the same man his father Allan Pinkerton had been.

He'd assigned Preston to the case, tasked him with ensuring that Blinder's factory was safe …

The carriage went over another bump in the road, and Violet's memory shifted again.

The small, seemingly unimportant notice she'd read in the business pages of the Chicago Tribune.

Blinder Patent Medicines acquires Silverman's Syrups.

She'd smelled a rat.

One of her favourite ploys in an investigation was to claim to be a newspaper reporter, and show up on the doorstep of a suspect, asking for an interview.

She'd been certain for as long as she could remember that people were fundamentally self-centred and selfish. If there were exceptions, she hadn't met many of them. But it still amazed her how many people—criminals especially—would jump at the invitation to talk about themselves. Especially if they thought it would buy them fifteen minutes of fame in a newspaper.

Dressed up as a reporter, she could ask and get answers to questions that would have got her thrown out the door if she'd gone in straight, as a Pinkerton's agent.

Well, she'd tried it on Blinder …

The cab bounced again. Violet gasped, and this time, whether by chance or strength of will, managed to open her eyes.

A tiny part of her had been hoping that this had all been a nightmare or some sort of bizarre hallucination. But no.

She really was sprawled on the dusty, grit-covered floor of a carriage.

And Urquhart—Urquhart really was her captor.

He hadn't seen her open her eyes yet. He was perched on the seat, doing something with a gauze pad and a brown glass bottle.

Violet swallowed down a wave of sickness and let her lids fall nearly closed again, looking through her lashes.

A large brown wicker hamper filled the other side of the coach. The shades were drawn down over the carriage windows, so that she couldn't see anything at all of the streets they were passing through or know where they were headed.

Violet breathed, going back—deliberately going back, this time—in her memory.

She'd learned all about Urquhart when she looked into Blinder and his Patent Medicines company.

Owen Urquhart was born in Drumnadrochit, Scotland, in the shadow of Urquhart Castle on the shores of Loch Ness. His parents supposedly had a family connection to the long-ruined and now deserted castle. They owned the village pharmacy and had prospered, opening a second and larger pharmacy in Inverness, that specialised in patent medicines.

Then, when Owen was fifteen, had come the tragic boating accident …

Urquhart replaced the glass bottle in a black leather bag, the kind that doctors carried. Violet tensed, ordering her muscles to be ready for a fight.

But either Urquhart was too fast or else she was still too slow. He must have seen whatever tiny movement she made, because his head swivelled in her direction, his wide mouth stretching in a smile.

"Wakin' up now, are ye?"

Before Violet could react, he clapped the wet pad onto her mouth and nose.

Violet choked, trying to struggle against his grip. But the darkness returned.

Chapter 3: Flynn

They were on the edge of the pavement in Piccadilly Circus, and Becky was holding his arm. Through the jumble of cabs and lorries and people milling about on the street, he could see the big black coach.

It was getting away, carrying Miss Violet Leverton, who was probably chloroformed and unconscious.

"Go back to Baker Street!" Flynn said.

Becky said just what he thought she'd say. "I'm coming with you."

But there wasn't time to argue. "No! Call Mr. Holmes!" he said.

Then he pulled his arm away and took off, pounding down the pavement as fast as his legs would take him, veering into the street and nearly colliding with a ragpicker's dog-cart piled high with old clothes. Flynn bounced off the side of the cart, running faster, passing the worn-out old horse and coming out ahead, until he could see his target.

A chance, he thought. If he ran as fast as he could …

But the big black coach was drawn by four big black horses, all fit and strong and well fed. They, too, were bucketing along as fast as they could down the busy street, sending other carts and cabs skittering to get out of the way. Flynn would have to keep that coach in sight and hope it stopped. Only then could he catch up and climb aboard.

So he had to keep that coach in sight. The life of Miss Violet

Leverton, the American lady who'd asked Flynn and Becky to help her recover a million dollars in bearer bonds not five minutes earlier, depended on it. He and Becky were waiting to follow her, as she'd instructed, when they saw someone grab her, clap a white cloth over her mouth—with a heavy dose of chloroform on the cloth, Flynn expected—and haul her inside.

Unless Flynn stayed with that coach to wherever it took Miss Leverton, he'd never be able to tell Mr. Holmes where she was. And Mr. Holmes had to be told.

Flynn wished he had a horse of his own. But the odds of anyone offering to lend a horse to a scraggly street boy on the spur of the moment were about equal to Flynn's own chances of sprouting wings and flying.

His break came just soon enough. His lungs felt like they were about to explode when, just as the coach was about to turn onto the Strand, a big furniture lorry came through and blocked the way. The coach stopped. Flynn legged it.

Now or never.

He reached the back, where a curved polished metal rail gleamed just below the seat a footman would be on, if there'd been a footman.

He reached up for the rail.

The coach started up again, lurching forwards, yanking the rail from his half-closed fingers.

He grabbed the base of the footman's seat and clung for dear life as the coach pulled him along. Pain burned though his shoulder and his wrist, but he held on, curling himself up, flailing around to get his feet onto the wooden storage platform notched into the base. He slid up onto the platform, still holding onto the footman's rail. He crouched down. The last thing he wanted was for someone on the street to notice him and call out to the driver. He hoped no one inside noticed the noise he'd made scrambling up. He hoped they wouldn't feel the increase in weight. He was just a scrawny kid, so it wasn't likely. But if they did, and if they slowed down to pull over, he knew he'd have to get away quick. He tensed, ready to jump at a moment's notice.

Chapter 4: Watson

Mycroft sat erect on our settee, dressed in his customary formal attire. His folded arms rested on his capacious waistcoat.

He said, "More work is required of you, Sherlock."

Holmes ignored the statement. Instead, he took the few steps required to reach our sideboard. "Mrs. Hudson has been hospitable," he said. "There is ice water in the carafe."

"I declined it," Mycroft said.

Holmes poured a glass for himself, gave me an inquiring glance, and then, at my nod, poured a second, which he handed to me. Still, he said nothing to his brother. The silence grew uncomfortable.

"The additional work you refer to—is it about the missing bonds?" I asked.

Mycroft was looking at Holmes. He said, "I do not mean the stolen bearer bonds, although their return to the United States Treasury would be appreciated."

"I shall be making a telephone call on that subject," Holmes said. "But first, where is the body?"

Mycroft sat silent. Once again, the silence became uncomfortable. I had the sense that the two brothers were intellectually jousting with one another, as was frequently the case when they met.

"Why should there be a body?" I asked.

"Because Mycroft is here," Holmes said. "Because normally he does not deviate from his self-appointed orbit between his rooms, the Diogenes Club, and his office in Whitehall. Yet today, a hot uncomfortable Sunday, with Parliament in its pre-election recess, Mycroft comes to Baker Street. He sends his cab away, and does not take refreshment, though it is offered by Mrs. Hudson and again by myself." He turned to Mycroft. "Come, now, brother. Nothing less than a matter of life and death would bring you here. And judging from the disturbance in Whitehall, which caused our cab to be interminably delayed as we travelled here from the station, the case has ramifications."

"The bodies are at St. Thomas's hospital," Mycroft said. "Two men, one woman. The Whitehall disturbance consists of an explosion and one ruined water-main, the principal source of water for Whitehall, including my office, my own personal flat, and the Diogenes Club. Repairs are in progress. The required excavations account for the disturbance to the flow of traffic. With an election coming, the ramifications of a Whitehall disturbance are indeed considerable, as you mention. Will you come?"

"Who is in charge for the police?"

"Gregson. Also, Commissioner Bradford has interested himself in the matter."

"As well he might. What do you know of the bodies?"

"Only that they were all memorable for the look of shock and horror on their faces."

I drew in my breath.

Holmes asked, "Where were they found?"

"On the street, near a manhole above the ruined water main."

"And you believe a bomb was dropped down the manhole?"

"Evidently. Witnesses heard a loud explosion."

"We must learn what we can."

Holmes stood and crossed over to our entry door. "Mrs. Hudson!" he called.

Our redoubtable landlady was with us a moment later. "Mr. Holmes?"

"Have we heard anything from a Miss Violet Leverton?"

She shook her head.

"Anything from a Mr. Preston, or from Lucy, Jack, Becky, or Flynn?"

"No, Mr. Holmes. Only Mr. Mycroft here."

"If one of them calls within the next hour, say we will meet them at 30 Pall Mall. The Junior Carlton Club."

Mycroft said, "That is not the location of the explosion."

"I did not say it was," Holmes replied. He looked expectantly at Mycroft.

"Ah," said Mycroft, nodding. "Your idea about the recovery of the stolen bonds."

"Indeed. The Junior Carlton is Galahad's club. We will go there after we visit the site of the explosion."

Holmes picked up the telephone once more.

Chapter 5: Becky

Flynn had told her to go back to Baker Street.

Baker Street was about two miles away from Piccadilly Circus. That would be at least twenty minutes. A cab would be quicker and might save valuable time.

But cab drivers would want to see money first, before taking on a young girl, and Becky had forgotten to bring any. She'd been walking for about ten minutes, resigned to a long walk on a hot day, with every lost moment giving more of a head start to whoever had kidnapped Miss Violet.

It hurt Becky to think of Miss Violet. With her hard-looking face, her soldier-like posture and jutting chin, the tall woman had been so determined and confident only a few minutes earlier, when she had told Flynn and Becky that she had a project on and needed their help. She'd strode off, and they'd followed at the distance she'd instructed. But then the black cab had pulled up and someone clamped that white cloth on Miss Violet's face, and Miss Violet had collapsed.

Becky and Flynn had run forward, but they were too far away and too slow. The kidnappers had dragged Miss Violet into that coach. Becky's last sight of her had been her sprawled-out legs, dangling, like those of a rag doll, disappearing into the recesses of the black coach.

Becky wished her brother Jack had been there.

Then she realised she was looking at a brick building, and at an angular blue lantern.

The lantern marked the entrance to the Carnaby Street police station.

The blue-painted wooden door was open. Inside, the floor and furniture were both in need of a sweep and a fresh varnish. She went up to the uniformed patrolman at the receiving desk.

"May I use your telephone, officer?"

Becky made her voice as grown up and polite as she could.

"I want to call my brother, Sergeant Jack Kelly," she went on. "It is a police matter, I assure you. My name is Becky Kelly. My brother is at Scotland Yard."

The desk sergeant gave her a long, appraising stare. "You want to call Scotland Yard?"

"No, actually at the moment my brother is with Mr. Sherlock Holmes at Baker Street. That's where I want to call."

"Do you know his number?"

"I do." And giving him the number of Mr. Holmes's telephone convinced him. A minute later she was behind the entry partition, standing on tiptoe at the station's wall telephone, holding the earpiece to her ear and talking up into the mouthpiece, first to the operator, and then to Mrs. Hudson.

Unfortunately, Mr. Holmes wasn't there, and neither was Dr. Watson.

But Mrs. Hudson gave her the address where they'd both gone. "Something to do with the Galahad case," Mrs. Hudson said. "On Pall Mall. Number 30. Junior Carlton Club. They only left a few minutes ago."

Becky's spirits rose. Whatever the Junior Carlton Club was, its address was just around the corner.

"I'll probably get there first!" she said.

CHAPTER 6: WATSON

We rode with Mycroft in a cab as far as the Diogenes Club. "I shall leave you here," he said. "The explosion occurred on Whitehall, not far from Trafalgar Square. It is only a few blocks away, but you will probably make better progress on foot. The roads are blocked for repairs, as I noted earlier."

The cab drew to a stop. Mycroft rapped for the cabman to open the door. Then he leaned forward. "Sherlock," he said, "you must understand the political implications. In barely a month's time, the election will be held, and its outcome will determine whether we achieve victory in South Africa or whether we suffer a defeat, lose the respect of the remainder of the Empire, and begin a period of inexorable decline in our Imperial powers. Bear in mind that this attack on British soil, in the heart of London, must be viewed as an act of war." He paused, and then added, "If the attack has been made by a foreign power, of course."

"I shall bear that in mind," Holmes said.

Then the cabman opened the door. Mycroft half-stood and pivoted his great bulk, grasping the hand rail and stepping down, ignoring the proffered arm of the waiting cabman.

The cabman looked at us, inquiring.

"Get us as close as you can to Trafalgar Square," Holmes said. "Go past, if possible. Stay on Whitehall."

When we were under way again, I asked, "What did he mean about the election and the war?"

"I take no interest in politics," he replied. "But it is certain that any breakdown in government service will be blamed on the incumbents."

I drew in my breath. "You are suggesting—"

"I suggest nothing, Watson. You know my methods."

"Yes, of course, only the facts, only the facts." I said. "But speaking hypothetically—"

"Then yes, hypothetically, cutting off the water supply of our city would be certain to arouse dissatisfaction with the current administration."

"And the citizens would express their dissatisfaction at the ballot box."

"They would vote out the incumbents. Hypothetically."

"I see. And since the incumbents support the war in South Africa and the opposition does not—"

"If the opposition won the election, a new administration would eventually withdraw our troops."

"As some Liberal candidates have already pledged to do."

"Correct." Holmes was looking out the window.

"So this act of sabotage would help the Boers defeat us."

"Hypothetically, yes. But the destruction of one water main is a small act in and of itself, even in the governmental command centre of the Empire. No doubt measures will be taken to keep the event out of the press."

"But if it were to be repeated—"

"Our cab is stopping. We must now leave the realm of speculation and get down to the facts of the case."

Chapter 7: Flynn

Flynn clung to his perch on the rail of the big black coach. It rattled over the Westminster Bridge, and then took a sharp turn, heading down to the river on the south side. Up ahead, waiting, was a green motor launch. Not a paddle-wheel affair, but one with a modern screw propeller beneath its stern, like one Flynn had seen on Lake Windermere. Above its polished metal smokestack, billows of grey smoke were floating upwards. Probably not coal, then. Probably diesel, Flynn thought. The kind of boat that could travel fast and far.

The coach was slowing down.

Time to jump, Flynn thought.

And he did. He found a spot behind a hedge where he could see the coach as it pulled alongside the river vessel.

The coachman climbed down from his driver's seat. Tall, broad-shouldered and with a well-trimmed black beard, he walked with a crisp, military bearing around to the door of the coach.

The door opened from inside.

Then a flat brown object filled the doorway. When it emerged, Flynn realised he was looking at the outside surface of a wicker hamper.

The coachman got his hands under the hamper and pulled. More of the container emerged. Then the coachman stepped away.

Another man, hollow-cheeked and shifty-eyed, dressed in black, came around from the other side of the coach and crouched next to the hamper. Flynn decided that this must be the man who had chloroformed Violet and dragged her into the coach. The second man gripped the bottom of the hamper and lifted, straightening his legs. He was thin, but evidently strong, for he moved smoothly, as if it were easy for him to take the hamper's weight. Together, he and the coachman pulled the hamper away from the coach and carried it down to the waiting green launch.

Of course, Miss Violet was inside the hamper, Flynn thought. They'd never have left her inside the coach. But just to be sure, he broke cover and ran to the still-open door on the far side of the coach. Flynn looked inside. The interior of the coach was empty. But beneath one of the tufted black leather seats, there was a paper crumpled on the floor.

Flynn picked up the paper and glanced at the writing. It was just a number.

52.

Flynn tucked the paper into his pocket. Then he looked up, through the other open coach door, down to the riverbank. He could see the green launch smokestack puffing smoke at a faster rate. The brown wicker hamper now sat squarely at the stern. The hollow-cheeked man stood in front of the hamper, talking to another man who stood at the boat's tiller. The coachman was leaving, stepping over the gunwale onto the landing dock. Flynn could see a pair of eyes, close-set and cold, framed by the well-trimmed black hair and beard, as the man strode towards him.

Fortunately, the coachman was looking at the horses. Till now they'd been quiet, taking a breather from their dash over here from Piccadilly Circus.

But in a few seconds the coachman would be standing next to Flynn.

Ducking down, Flynn picked up a stone and tossed it at the flank of one of the four black horses. It whinnied and stamped, setting the other three to moving about.

"Settle down, you," the coachman said. "You're not done yet."

While the man was busy with the horses, Flynn scrambled back to the clump of bushes where he'd been hiding. Not spotted, that was good. But now he had to decide. Which should he follow? The coach might lead to the villain's lair. But the boat, he knew, had Miss Violet on board, and she was helpless. Likely drugged again, with another dose of ether or whatever had been on that white cloth.

Making up his mind, he edged towards the riverbank where the bushes no longer grew, down at the water line. He waited. The coachman, his horses under control again, shut both doors and climbed up to his driver's box. The coach drove off.

The two men on the motor launch watched the coach. Flynn scuttled, crab-wise, till he was behind the wicker hamper.

There wasn't room on the deck, but there were a few inches between the back wall of the boat and the hamper, which, fortunately, screened Flynn from the two others. He eased himself up and squeezed into the narrow space.

The boat came away from the dock. River water, stagnant and smelly, sloshed over the side and onto Flynn's boots. The hollow-faced man tossed his pole down. It made a clatter on the deck. The chuff-chuff of the engine sped up and grew louder, the smoke billowed thicker, and Flynn had to cover his face and hold his breath to keep from coughing.

He pressed his face against the rough surface of the hamper, hoping to see if Miss Violet was still alive. But the wicker was too thick.

Where were they going? Because of the crumpled note he'd found in the coach, he thought they were headed for somewhere in the Docklands, where there were at least 52 docks.

He settled down to wait.

Chapter 8: Watson

Across the pavement, beneath the grand stately towers of Whitehall, Inspector Tobias Gregson had stationed several uniformed patrolmen to keep order. They had spread themselves on the perimeter surrounding the manhole where the explosion had originated. The top of a ladder was visible above the manhole. Closer to the centre of this protected work area, workmen busied themselves unloading several dog-carts piled high with bricks and carrying them in their familiar wooden hods. Two more workers stood by a wide metal pan, making concrete for the bricklayers by mixing sand and cement with the water from several buckets that sat nearby. Yet another stood by a fire department water truck, filling more buckets with water.

Fortunately, Gregson was still at hand. The inspector was fanning himself with his hat against the July heat. The sunlight gleamed on his close-cropped blond hair. His face was ruddy and perspiring.

He caught sight of us and lifted a hand in greeting. "Mr. Holmes. Dr. Watson."

"You look well, Gregson," I told him after returning his greeting. "Marriage clearly agrees with you. And how is your wife?"

We had witnessed Gregson and a former suspect in one of our cases united in marriage not long ago.

"Amy is well," Gregson answered. "She's staying with my parents for the moment, until the baby comes."

"That is good news. My heartiest congratulations." I clapped Gregson on the shoulder.

"Thank you."

Holmes had been fidgeting with impatience throughout these pleasantries. Gregson had worked with us on several cases and Holmes held his abilities and temperament in high esteem, but that did not increase Holmes's tolerance for small talk centred around Gregson's personal life.

"What time did the explosion occur?" Holmes asked.

"Hard to say, one way or the other. The witnesses weren't observing the time. Three victims were near the manhole. Two men and a woman. Nobody paid them attention. Then someone noticed that they were all lying motionless on the pavement. The explosion was underground, so the sound was muffled. We got the call just after noon."

"How far from the manhole?"

"Perhaps ten feet. Not far from the curb. That was when we arrived, of course. They may have been moved."

"Their positions?"

"Face down, arms outstretched. We thought they had been flung away by the force of the explosion."

"Pointing in which direction?"

"What?"

"The bodies. Which way were their arms pointing?" Holmes was beginning to sound testy.

"Ah. Let me recollect." Gregson took off his hat and ran his fingers through his hair. Then he replaced his hat. "I do remember. They were all three alongside the road, pointing in the direction of the Yard."

"Scotland Yard, you mean?" I asked.

"Yes."

"Were all three in a line, one behind the other?"

"All in a row, they were."

"Pointing which way, in relation to the manhole?"

"In front of it. And away, of course. Though they were off to the side, as I said."

"Excellent, Gregson. Where is the manhole cover?"

Gregson pointed to the perimeter of the roadway, where uniformed patrolmen stood, legs spread, brandishing truncheons to keep the area clear of pedestrians and vehicles. The manhole cover lay beside one of the patrolmen. Its heavy cast iron was shaped in a thick rectangle, very nearly square, with moulded lettering that proclaimed it to be the property of the Southwark Vauxhall Company.

"Southwark supplies the water for this area," Holmes said. "Watson, will you help me turn it over?"

We knelt and lifted, keeping to the outer rim, at Holmes's insistence, to avoid the finger-holes on each side. The cover was two inches thick and surprisingly heavy, but together we had no difficulty raising it upon its edge.

"Let it fall over so we can observe the underside," Holmes said. "Careful of your fingers." We did so. The resultant clatter caused heads to turn, but only for a moment.

Holmes stretched out prone, as if he were doing a press-up exercise, his hands beneath his shoulders. He sniffed at the perimeter, and looked carefully at both finger-holes. "The grime of a decade or two is here, coated with what appears to be explosive residue."

"Dynamite smoke?" came a familiar voice.

We turned to see Preston, the Pinkerton man. In his

shirtsleeves, his coat slung over one arm, he still wore the string tie with the long-horn cow's head. His blue eyes twinkled.

"Thought I'd find you here," he said. "I stopped by your place and your landlady said you'd gone to Whitehall. Might have known you'd be at the scene of the trouble."

Holmes continued to inspect the manhole cover. "A moment," he said.

Gregson came over and I performed introductions.

"I came back with your friend Lestrade," Preston said.

"He told me he was going up to Tottenham," Gregson said. "The American bond case."

"We looked all over for those bonds. Tore Calloway's place apart. Also Galahad's living quarters. Didn't find anything."

Holmes, kneeling now, lifted the manhole cover upon its edge once again. He pointed to the side that contained the company name. "There is of course explosive residue on the underside," he said. "But here on the upper surface appears to be charring around this one finger-hole aperture."

Gregson said, "Then the sequence seems plain enough. The cover was lifted by the two men. A fuse leading to the bomb was threaded through the aperture, so as to protrude above the cover. That would have been the woman's work. The bomb was lowered to the bottom of the manhole, where the water pipes run. The cover was replaced. The fuse was lit. The explosion blew the manhole cover off and knocked all three people across the road."

"A powerful blast," I said. "But how to account for the expressions on the faces of the three bodies?"

"Probably the fuse burned faster than they expected. In the last instant, they realised what was happening, but too late,"

Gregson said. "They all tried to fling themselves clear, and wound up along the side of the road."

"But why didn't they just walk away right after they lit the fuse?" Preston said. "After all, that's what a fuse is for."

"We shall learn more at the mortuary," Holmes said. He got to his feet.

"I'll have the police van take you over to St. Thomas Hospital," Gregson said. "I'll need to stay here till the workmen finish."

Holmes nodded his thanks. "I hope the bodies have not been manipulated in any way?"

"You will find them just as we found them. Clothed. I gave instructions on that point."

"Excellent, again, Inspector."

As we were about to board the van, Holmes said. "Mr. Preston, would you care to accompany us? I propose a quick stop along the way. That destination is close at hand and it pertains to the other case."

CHAPTER 9: FLYNN

The launch turned sooner than Flynn had anticipated, just after they had passed under Tower Bridge. The pilot had passed a large yacht then immediately swung right into a narrow channel. Up ahead tall dirty brick buildings rose up on either side of what looked like a harbour, with a decrepit wooden quay extending as far as Flynn could see. The place didn't seem too busy that day, probably because it was Sunday.

Flynn wondered if this was the place referred to on the crumpled paper note now in Flynn's pocket, the one with the 52 docks.

Flynn risked a peek around the other side of the hamper. He didn't see fifty-two docks. Only four or five, and all where he was, close to the mouth of the channel.

An old scow floated just twenty feet away from Flynn. The paint on its rusted and lifeless smoke stack had long ago lost its original green colour and now its flaked surface hung like clumps of dirty moss. The deck of the scow was only a foot or so above Flynn's eye level. But there was a number in fresh white paint on the peeling hull.

52

The launch was coming closer.

"All right, get alongside and hoist her over," came a rough voice.

Flynn didn't wait. He slid noiselessly off the stern, into the brackish, foul-smelling harbour waters, and made for the wooden pillars beneath the dock. He held onto the rough, splintered surface, watching and looking for his chance to pull up and roll onto the planking.

Chapter 10: Becky

30 Pall Mall was one in a row of tall grey limestone buildings. Huge arched windows loomed above Becky as she stood on the pavement, wondering what was behind the darkened curtains visible behind the many panes of glass. There was a big black door between two of the windows, with a concrete archway that matched the windows on either side. The number '30' had been cast in concrete at the top of the arch. There was no doorman.

Becky wondered. Was this the building where Miss Violet planned to come? Where Miss Violet had warned her and Flynn that they were on no account to go inside?

Becky pushed the door open. She saw several doors along a hallway, like a hotel or a row of doctors' offices. There were brass plaques on each of the doors, shiny and rectangular. One of them read 'Junior Carlton Club.'

She tried pushing on that door, but it was locked.

Becky knocked. Knocked again.

The door swung open to reveal a grey-haired gentleman in a grey flannel uniform suit, with gold trim like a soldier's or a military guard's. His blue eyes registered first annoyance, then surprise, then amusement.

"We're members-only, Miss," he said.

"I'm waiting for someone."

"Is he a member?"

She thought furiously. A club. Was Mr. Holmes a member? Probably not. But he was coming here. Why? What was he working on? The answer came to her, and she said, "Yes. Mr. Galahad Trent. Lord Trent."

"Indeed, Miss. And you say he is coming here to meet you?"

"That's right."

"Coming here, himself?"

Becky had the feeling that she was walking across a lake of ice and that the ice was cracking beneath her feet. "I'm not sure. He might be sending someone."

"To pick up a package?"

"That's right."

The man nodded, satisfied. "We did have a telephone message to that effect. In fact, two messages."

Behind them, the outer door opened. Becky could hear the street noise. She turned, expecting to see Mr. Holmes. But instead she saw a tall man dressed in black, wearing a bowler hat. A black scarf hung from his broad shoulders. His face was flat and hard, clean-shaven, with bulging muscles at his jaws.

"I've come for Lord Trent's package," he said.

Becky stepped back, involuntarily.

The man in grey said, "Right you are, sir. We've been expecting you. Just one moment."

He ducked back behind the door, leaving Becky face to face with the black-clad man.

Becky had the urge to run. She had a feeling that this man could be one of the gang who had kidnapped Miss Violet.

But Becky knew the man wouldn't recognise her. No one

had noticed her during the abduction. "Yes, Lord Trent said he would be here later," she said. "I came to meet him. I'm his ward," she added.

The man didn't bother to hide his disinterest. He turned back to the partially opened door. Which was just fine with Becky.

A moment later the man in the grey uniform returned, holding a manila envelope about the size of a folded-up newspaper. He smiled. The man in black reached for it. The man in grey stood still.

"The telephone message said you would give a name, sir."

"Of course," the man growled. "Patterson. The name's Patterson. Is this the only package?"

"Indeed, it is."

"I'll have it, then."

"I'll inform Lord Trent when he arrives," said the man in grey, and handed over the envelope.

The other man tucked it into his jacket without looking. He turned away, adjusted his bowler hat, and strode towards the exit.

Becky watched him go. A growler cab was at the curb, and he got in. The cab did not move. She could see the man through the window, bent over the envelope, looking at papers.

Her insides swirled. Should she follow the man, or wait for Mr. Holmes? The man had something important in that envelope, that was certain, if Galahad wanted it to be picked up. Was Galahad somehow mixed up with this man? Was the man calling himself Patterson one of Miss Violet's kidnappers?

Unlikely, she thought. Very unlikely. It had been nearly half an hour since she had seen the black coach only a few blocks from here, driving away faster than she could run.

She didn't know those answers.

But she did know she needed to tell Mr. Holmes that Miss Violet had been kidnapped, and that Flynn had gone after her.

She decided to wait outside on the street and watch for Mr. Holmes. She could also, she thought, keep an eye on the cab.

Chapter 11: Violet

Violet heard voices and felt the ground shift beneath her.

No, not the ground. Sharp points jabbed her from all sides, the small pricks of pain bringing her back to consciousness.

Urquhart must have stuffed her inside the wicker hamper she'd seen inside the carriage, and now she was being lifted. Carried.

She could hear grunts from the men alongside her, but when she opened her eyes, the wicker was too thick to catch a glimpse of who they were or where they were taking her.

She felt a sickening lurch. She and the hamper were falling, falling … and then the impact with something hard and unyielding came, snapping her head back and jarring her bones.

She'd barely managed to get her brain to stop rattling when the hamper tilted, and they poured her out like a basket of fish.

The ropes of a mouldy cargo net scraped her cheek and filled her nose and mouth with the vile stench of mud and old fish. Then the net was yanked out from beneath her and she rolled onto the dirty, smelly boards of what she realised was some kind of ship.

Violet gritted her teeth, got her feet underneath her, and managed to stand. Her vision shimmered and her muscles shook, but at least she was no longer sprawled on the floor like the day's catch.

She was inside a cabin of sorts, with rough wooden walls all around on three sides and a corrugated tin roof overhead. A slender man stood outside the entrance, his back to her, lifting a thick hawser cable from a hook attached to the cabin.

The cable came loose and fell to the deck with a clatter. Beneath it was the cargo net, now a heap of tangled ropes.

Looking beyond the man and through the cabin door, she could see that the ship was in a canal. Tall warehouse buildings rose up on either side. A few dozen yards away were the pillars and boards of grey wooden docks. Coal smoke rose from the stack of a smaller vessel—a fast steam launch, she realised—that was pulled alongside their boat. A burly man on the deck of the launch was tugging at the far end of the hawser cable.

Then the man in the cabin door turned around, focusing on her.

Urquhart.

"Awake now, are ye?"

Violet's palms felt cold and slick with sweat, but somehow she felt strong inside, and she certainly wasn't going to give Urquhart the satisfaction of letting him know that she was afraid.

"How observant of you."

Urquhart's lip curled. He stepped into the cabin, pulling the door shut behind him. "Think you're smart, don't ye?"

She was now shut in here with Urquhart, in a space so small that one step would bring him close enough that he'd be able to grab her. He was also entirely blocking a path to the door, her only escape route.

And there was no chance that anyone would hear her—or care—if she screamed.

"I don't just think that I'm intelligent," Violet said calmly. "I know that I am."

Urquhart didn't like that answer. Like most bullies, he liked his victims to cower suitably before him.

His face reddened a shade, and his jaw flexed.

"Oh, aye? Ye weren't so smart back in America. Tried to go after Blinder and where'd it get ye? Tossed straight out of Pinkerton's."

That, unfortunately for Violet, was an accurate summary.

Mr. Pinkerton had found out about her visit to Blinder under her newspaper reporter's cover story. She'd been summarily hauled into his office, charged with working a case for personal reasons—and, worse, working against a client—and fired.

Urquhart's lip curled back. "How does it feel to know you gave up everything for Preston, and he still won't look at you?"

In a way, he couldn't have said anything more helpful, because Violet actually laughed at that.

Urquhart might be an excellent research chemist, but he didn't have much skill at reading people. Even before she'd lost her position at Pinkerton's, Beau Preston was the last man on earth who would have looked at her with romantic designs, or she him.

Although she probably had him to thank, at least partly, for her success as an agent. They'd competed and rivalled each other to solve cases, and her determination not to be outdone by Preston had driven her to excel.

She faced Urquhart, who was looking put out again by her laughter.

"How does it feel to have murdered your parents?" Violet asked.

A flicker in Urquhart's eyes told her that the shot had gone home. She'd been reasonably sure, even if she couldn't prove that the deaths of Urquhart's father and mother lay at his door.

All the official records showed was that while on a family boating expedition on Loch Ness, Urquhart's parents had tragically fallen overboard and drowned. The fifteen-year-old Owen had stayed with the boat, called for help from a passing launch, and been rescued.

But when Mr. Pinkerton had fired Violet, he couldn't take away her instincts or skills as an investigator. And she'd been extremely motivated to learn everything she could about Urquhart and Blinder, both.

Having inherited his parents' property and pharmacy business, Urquhart had gone to university in London, then emigrated to America and got a job in Blinder's patent medicine factory as a chemist.

"What did your other murder victim have on Mr. Blinder?" Violet asked. "Did he know some inconvenient truths about Blinder's business practices? Or have information about the safety of his so-called medicines?"

Urquhart blinked, then recovered. "Done yer homework, haven't ye?"

Violet leaned in just a little. "You were sloppy, though. Got yourself caught and arrested for murder."

She had read the police report herself. Mr. Pinkerton hadn't been able to take away Violet's handful of useful contacts within the police force, either.

On the night of September 21st, 1898, Owen Urquhart had killed a Mr. Thomas Pryde in what he'd claimed was an act of self-defence.

Mr. Pryde was a former employee at Blinder's factory, and Urquhart's claim had been that when Pryde was dismissed for drunkenness on the job, he'd come back in a drunken rage to attack everyone who still worked for Blinder.

But if the Chicago police force weren't exactly on the level of Sherlock Holmes, even their suspicions had been roused by the lack of any alcohol in Pryde's system at the time of his death.

"I doubt Mr. Blinder was particularly happy that he had to pay one of his expensive lawyers to get you out of jail and have the charges against you dropped," Violet said. "I'm surprised he still lets you run his errands for him. Although I suppose most pet owners value obedience in their dogs more than they do intelligence."

"You—" Urquhart's face flushed red, and he lunged for her.

Which was exactly the reaction Violet had been hoping to provoke.

As Urquhart came at her, she caught his wrist and used his momentum to jerk him forward and pull his arm straight out.

Shock flashed across Urquhart's face, but he didn't have time to react. Violet twisted his arm up, then drove the heel of her palm into Urquhart's elbow. She heard the dry pop of the joint dislocating even above Urquhart's howl of pain.

But she was already moving, shoving him to the ground in her race for the cabin door.

The door swung open, revealing a burly man—the same man who'd been adjusting the hawser cable on the steam launch. But now Violet could see his face.

Blinder.

She had a half second to debate whether she could disable him, too. But then he pulled a pistol from his belt, levelling it at her.

He might have been eyeing an insect he was about to swat.

"Where are the bonds?" he asked.

Violet dragged in a breath. Disappointment choked her, and

the lingering effect of the chloroform was making her stomach churn and her head throb. She shoved it all aside.

"I might tell you," she said.

On the cabin floor, Urquhart moaned in pain, cradling his arm. Blinder flicked him a scornful glance but made no move to help.

"So, tell me."

"If you take me to a public place in a better part of town, and then set me free."

Blinder grinned. "Not at the moment."

Violet hadn't really expected him to take the bargain, but it had been worth trying. She raised her eyebrows. "One million dollars and you're not interested?"

"You fancy yourself a clever lady, do you?"

"Prove me wrong."

"Your client is dead."

That was true. Although Blinder's former partner, Allan Brown, hadn't been much of a client. Violet had known he was crooked. She'd taken his job and his money solely because she'd hoped it would lead her to the stolen bearer bonds—and thus give her a chance to land Brown, Urquhart, and Blinder all three in jail.

"And?" she said.

"Calloway killed him. We saw the police at Galahad's Castle, leading him away in handcuffs."

"You may be right," she said. "But you still don't know where the bonds are now."

Blinder didn't even bother to smile or gloat, just kept looking at her coldly. The expression made a chill dash down Violet's spine. He wouldn't be nearly as easy to manipulate as Urquhart had been.

"We put ourselves into Calloway's place," Blinder said. "He would expect the Castle and his home to be searched. So, he would mail them to himself, somewhere else. We deduced that he mailed them to Galahad's club, intending to pick them up before Galahad got there. So, if we're correct, the bonds are still at the club. That was where you were going when we picked you up, wasn't it?"

"But what if you're not correct?"

She was still bluffing, of course, but tried to keep that from showing. In retrospect, the deduction had been fairly simple, all things considered.

"We've sent a man there. He will soon return. When he does, we will know if we need to interview you further."

"Preston knows where I am," Violet said.

It was a last-ditch effort at bluffing, and unfortunately Blinder knew it. He didn't even pause to consider before giving a dismissive snort.

"Preston's got enough to worry about with that sister of his." He gave Urquhart another scornful look and kicked him with the toe of his boot. "Get up."

Urquhart's breath was still ragged, but he scrambled unsteadily to his feet.

"Tie her." Blinder jerked his chin at a pile of rope on the cabin floor.

"I—" Urquhart swallowed, his dislocated arm dangling uselessly.

Blinder's eyes narrowed. "Serves you right for letting her get the better of you."

Urquhart cringed. "Yes, sir."

"Fine. I'll do it myself."

Violet's heart skipped in momentary hope. But unfortunately

for her, it took Blinder only a fraction of a second to pass the gun over to Urquhart.

Urquhart might be in pain, but he could still aim a weapon. In a space this small, he wouldn't even need particularly *good* aim to hit her if he pulled the trigger. She still didn't dare move.

Blinder bent to retrieve the ropes. "When we know whether the bonds were at the club, we can decide whether she's worth further attention. Until then—"

He refocused on Violet, his gaze indifferent enough to send a fresh jolt of ice through her.

He could order Urquhart to shoot her, toss her body overboard, and care about it no more than if he'd just killed a gnat.

He probably would do exactly that, unless she could find a reason for him to keep her alive between now and whenever his employee returned.

"Until then, you can cool your heels in here."

Chapter 12: Becky

Becky did not have long to wait at the Junior Carlton Club.

The cab she had been watching had just driven off and the man with the bowler hat was still inside. Then another four-wheeler cab drove up, and Sherlock Holmes opened the door. Becky could see Dr. Watson behind him and Preston, the Pinkerton detective.

"Stay inside," Becky said. She climbed up. "There's a cab we have to follow."

Holmes rapped on the panel and gave orders to the driver.

Once they were under way, Becky explained.

CHAPTER 13: VIOLET

Violet lay on the cabin floor, breathing in the smell of mouldy fish and water-logged wood. Blinder had tied the ropes tight enough to cut into her skin. Her wrists were secured behind her back and her ankles were lashed together.

Trussed up like a Christmas turkey, a voice that sounded suspiciously like Preston's drawled in her mind. *Not good, Leverton, not good at all.*

Violet hated to let even an imaginary version of Preston get the last word. But he was right. She'd got herself into this predicament, and short of a miracle, she was coming up depressingly short of ideas on how to get herself out again.

In sensational fiction, there was always a handy nail or a shard of broken glass for the hero to rub his bonds against until the ropes frayed and snapped.

The ship's cabin floor was devoid of anything useful like that. From where she lay, Violet could see three mouldering scraps of fishing net, the stub of a broken pencil, and a wad of crumpled newspaper. Nothing at all that would help her cut through her bonds, which meant that she had nothing to do but lie here, with Urquhart's words ringing in her ears.

You gave up everything for Preston.

She hadn't. Not really. She certainly hadn't gone after Blinder because she had romantic feelings for Preston.

Certainly not. She was a female detective working alone in a man's world. She couldn't afford to let herself smile at a fluffy kitten or a rosy-cheeked child, much less indulge in anything as sloppily sentimental as falling in love.

And falling in love with Preston, of all people—

His face flashed before her: lean and sun-bronzed, with half-lidded eyes and his trademark lazy, slightly sardonic smile.

She wasn't even going to consider the possibility that she might have feelings for him apart from annoyance mingled with the occasional dash of grudging professional respect.

Whatever else he might be, Preston was an excellent Pinkerton's agent. Behind his slow nonchalance and southern drawl there was a razor-sharp intelligence and a ruthless drive to catch whatever criminal he was after.

Right now, though, Violet's mind kept carrying her back to the night when she'd happened, purely by chance, to see Preston buying eggs and oranges at the corner store near her own rented apartment.

The mundane, ordinary activity felt utterly at odds with what she knew of Preston's character. Men like Preston exchanged gunfire with Chicago street gangs and leaped onto the roof of moving railway cars to foil train robberies. They didn't carry out trivial housekeeping errands.

She'd said as much to Preston, sarcastically. Sarcasm was practically the only common language she and Preston shared.

But instead of coming back with an equally sardonic reply, Preston had looked momentarily weary, and told her that the eggs and oranges were for his sister, who was an invalid and couldn't do her own shopping.

He hadn't said as much, but Violet had formed the impression that Preston was his sister's sole means of financial support, too.

She'd been surprised to hear Preston was capable of caring for anyone besides himself. Surprised, and a little touched that a man who was as much of a lone wolf as Preston had hidden feelings of family loyalty.

Then grimness had overshadowed Preston's expression once more, and he'd gone on to say that his sister had been one of the factory workers at Silverman's to fall ill with mysterious symptoms.

Maybe she had been motivated at least partially by that conversation when she'd decided that Mr. Blinder's affairs were worthy of investigating.

And then had come the confrontation in Mr. Pinkerton's office—

Voices from outside the cabin caught her ear. Urquhart and Blinder, talking.

Violet silently cursed herself. Instead of lying sprawled here on the ground, wallowing in self-pity, she could have been seizing this chance to listen in on Blinder's plans.

She couldn't get to her feet or even sit up, but she managed to wriggle, worm-like, until she was pressed up against the cabin's decaying wall. Even better, there was a chink in between the splintering boards, through which she could see both Blinder and Urquhart.

They were on the deck, their heads bent together over something they seemed to be studying, but she couldn't see whatever it was.

Blinder was speaking. "First, I want results from the lock." He might have caught sight of something, then, because he looked up sharply, his gaze focused on a point outside of Violet's narrow field of view. "He's coming."

Urquhart nodded. He still looked a little on the greenish-pale side, his arm hung in a makeshift sling and cradled protectively across his chest.

"Moment of truth," he replied.

Chapter 14: Flynn

Flynn saw it all from his hiding place on the dock.

They'd used a cargo net and a hawser to sling the wicker hamper from the green launch onto the deck of the scow. Then Miss Violet had come out of the hamper.

Flynn was glad to see that Miss Violet appeared to be all right, for she stood up and talked to them, briefly. The larger of the two, who Flynn named Mr. Big, held a gun on her till they were done talking. Then the skinnier of the two men, who Flynn named Skinny, hustled her inside the cabin. Mr. Big followed, with the gun in his hand.

A few minutes later, both men came back out, and Flynn noticed that one of Skinny's arms was dangling uselessly at his side. Had Violet done that? Flynn hoped Violet had not been harmed, but only locked inside the cabin.

Now Mr. Big and Skinny had their heads bent, looking at something. Flynn didn't know what it could be. He was thinking how to get closer but then a water taxi, a little paddle steamer, came into view. The water taxi stopped alongside the old scow.

For a moment Flynn couldn't see what was happening, because the water taxi blocked his vision. But then the boat pulled away and Flynn saw a man in a black suit and bowler hat standing on the deck of the scow.

The man had a tan envelope in his hand. Flynn named him

the Messenger, and figured that he planned to stay, since the paddleboat was now out of sight.

Mr. Big held out his hand for the envelope. He took the envelope and started talking to the Messenger, turning so that the backs of both men were to the cabin.

Skinny came out from behind the cabin. One of his arms was in a sling.

Skinny was carrying something in his other hand. He was holding it down by his right leg. Neither Mr. Big nor the Messenger seemed to notice. Skinny waited behind the Messenger.

Flynn could see what Skinny was concealing. It was a long-handled ax, the kind firemen use.

Mr. Big opened the envelope. He inspected the contents for some time.

Then he held out the envelope, opening it so the Messenger could inspect what was inside. Flynn guessed it was money.

The Messenger bent over to look.

Mr. Big leaned away, and Skinny came up from behind with the ax. Before the Messenger could straighten up, Skinny swung the axe in a roundhouse blow, a bit awkwardly, since one of his arms was in the sling, but the head of the axe caught the Messenger directly on the side of the head. Flynn could hear the crack of the impact across the water.

The Messenger crumpled.

Mr. Big turned the Messenger's body over with his foot. He crouched down and pulled a piece of paper from the Messenger's jacket pocket. He tucked the paper into the envelope, and then nodded to the skinny man.

The skinny man dragged the Messenger off to the side of the cabin.

CHAPTER 15: VIOLET

Violet's heart pounded, and her mouth tasted of bitter metal. Through the crack in the cabin wall, she saw Blinder's messenger crumple bonelessly to the deck, blood pooling under his head from the axe wound. His mouth hung open and his sightless eyes seemed to stare straight into Violet's.

Urquhart looked down at the dead man, satisfaction stamped on his narrow face, and the thought flicked across Violet's mind that he'd enjoyed this. Killing the messenger must have felt like a chance to get a bit of his own back, after the humiliation of being attacked and disabled by a mere woman.

Violet squeezed her eyes shut, trying to fight back a wave of sickness.

What's the matter, Leverton? Preston's imaginary voice spoke in her mind again. *Going to let a little thing like watching a murder bother you?*

Violet opened her eyes. *I'm fine. I **wish** that man's death was the worst thing I'd ever seen.*

She clearly wasn't fine, or she wouldn't be conversing with a figment of her own imagination. But the thought still steadied her. She had seen uglier sights and lived through worse days than this one.

Urquhart moved, disappearing from Violet's field of view. For a second, she didn't know where he'd gone, and then she heard the squelch of his footsteps on the damp wooden deck boards, approaching her cabin.

She had just enough time to roll and wriggle away from the crack in the wall before the cabin door swung open.

Not that she likely had much to lose if Urquhart knew that she'd been spying on them, but she had acted purely on instinct.

Urquhart stood in the doorway of the cabin. He was smiling, and he still carried the bloodied axe in his good hand.

Violet swallowed hard.

Urquhart swung the axe to and fro. "Didn't know what ye were getting into, did ye, Miss Nosey?"

Fear scrambled in Violet's chest. Under ordinary circumstances, she didn't fear Urquhart nearly as much as she did Blinder. But a deadly weapon in the hands of a man with a grudge wasn't a good combination. And the cold, stark truth was that she was still tied up and completely helpless if Urquhart decided to attack.

"Got a score to settle with you." Urquhart kept swinging the axe back and forth, like the supposedly hypnotic watch in a cheap magician's act.

"An axe to grind, you mean?" The moment the words were out, Violet wondered why for once in her life she couldn't have just kept quiet. Avoided antagonising the man with the bloodied ax. That would have been a good idea.

Urquhart's face twisted with anger and he took a menacing step towards her. "Got a smart mouth, don't ye? I'll wager you won't sound nearly so sure of yerself if I chop off a finger or two."

Violet clamped her jaw shut.

Then Blinder's shout came from outside. "It's time! Get out here!"

Urquhart startled, glanced reflexively over his shoulder, then returned his gaze to Violet.

"Too bad you won't be around to see what happens next."

He swung the axe in a wide, overhand arc. The blade whistled through the air. Violet just barely managed not to squeeze her eyes shut.

The axe head sunk into the cabin floor, a foot or so away from her.

Urquhart spun on his heel, striding out of the cabin and slamming the door shut behind him.

Violet exhaled a long, shuddering breath. Her muscles wanted to go slack with relief, but she couldn't afford that now. From outside, she could hear the steady rumble of a steam-launch engine, probably carrying Urquhart and Blinder away.

But unwittingly or not, Urquhart had just left her with a possible means to free herself. If she could just manoeuvre herself into position to pry the axe loose from the floorboards, she might be able to use it to cut through her bonds, like all those heroines in sensational fiction—

The deafening boom of an explosion punched the air, so loud that Violet felt its impact as an almost physical force, compressing the air around her. The ship lurched, then tipped violently to one side, so that she rolled helplessly all the way across the cabin—away from the ax—and finally came to rest with her nose against the opposite wall.

This day just gets better and better, doesn't it, Leverton? the imaginary Preston drawled inside her head.

But this time, Violet didn't come up with an answer. A torrent of icy, brackish water was pouring into the cabin from under the door, soaking her hair and clothes in seconds. She only just managed to roll sideways to avoid getting any in her mouth.

The ship was sinking. Fast.

Chapter 16: Flynn

The green launch was still alongside the scow.

Flynn saw the wisps of smoke from the stack turn to puffs, and then to black and grey clouds, billowing upwards. Something was going on.

Mr. Big emerged from the bridge, walking quickly. He stopped at the edge of the scow and looked down. He turned back and yelled something. Then he clambered over the side, gripping the hawser rope. He swung outwards, sliding down onto the deck of the steam launch.

Skinny followed him a moment later and awkwardly, with his one working arm, helped the other man fling the hawser rope out of the launch.

The launch moved away, smoke streaming from its smokestack, headed towards the mouth of the harbour.

It picked up speed.

It was nearly out of sight when Flynn heard a loud bang. He saw foam and waves on the water, next to the old scow.

The old scow shuddered and rocked. Then it tilted to one side. The hawser rope dangled from the other side. The scow tilted more, and faster.

Bloody 'ell, she's sinking! Flynn swore under his breath. Then he broke from his hiding place in the bushes. He took a run and a flying leap. A moment later he realised he'd kept his boots on, but there wasn't time to stop. He set his sights on the dangling hawser rope and swam for all he was worth.

As he clambered on board, he could hear someone moving inside Miss Violet's cabin.

When he broke down the door, she was knee-deep in water, trying to rub the ropes on her wrists against the blade of the ax.

Chapter 17: Becky

Flynn looked like a drowned rat. He sat on the deck of the water taxi, his legs crossed, picking at his shoelaces. The taxi boat was headed for Westminster Bridge. Puddles from his soaked coat and trousers spread out around him.

Miss Violet looked bad too. Mr. Preston was holding her. He was trying to get her to drink from a flask Dr. Watson had given him, but she was turning her face away. Becky could see strands of her dark hair plastered across her forehead and her cheeks.

Becky nudged Flynn and pointed to the spot on the river where they'd found him and Miss Violet struggling to stay afloat.

"I thought you could swim better than that," she said to Flynn. He still looked a bit pale, and ragging him was usually her best antidote for being scared. For a few horrible seconds, she'd thought he was going to drown.

"What happens when a big boat sinks," he said. "Suction takes you down. And we were ten feet under to start with."

"You need help with your shoelaces?"

Flynn gave her a look.

Mr. Holmes came over to stand beside them, his eyes on the dock up ahead, beside Westminster Bridge. "You are both to be congratulated on your initiative," he said. "Miss Leverton owes her life to you."

"Do you want to hear what happened?" Becky asked.

"Later. We will meet at 221B Baker Street to review events and plan our course of action. I will alert the police. Gregson and Lestrade, if they are available. Lucy and Jack as well."

At the taxi dock, Preston was the first to leap out. He hailed a cab. "It'll hold six," he said. "Baker Street?"

Holmes nodded. "Yes, for the four of you."

"You're not coming?"

"Dr. Watson and I must walk across the bridge to St. Thomas Hospital," Mr. Holmes said. "We shall return to Baker Street when we can. Kindly wait for us. Becky, can you please tell Mrs. Hudson that refreshments would be welcome. Also, dry clothes."

"Mine will dry soon enough," Flynn said.

Chapter 18: Watson

It was late afternoon when we arrived at St. Thomas Hospital. I was tired and dusty from our walk across the bridge. As we entered the stairwell leading down to the mortuary, a janitor, grey and stooped and twisted, was laboriously ascending the stairs, his mop and bucket clanking against his side. I felt a moment's pity for the old fellow. My own discomfort seemed petty by comparison.

Gregson was waiting for us outside the door. His Nordic features showed his own fatigue, but his characteristic enthusiasm was still evidenced by the gleam in his blue eyes. "The water main is repaired," he said. "Commissioner Bradford is inside."

Despite the July weather, the Commissioner appeared unruffled, his white hair and moustache immaculate. His neatly tailored suit was beginning to wilt, however, although its empty left sleeve, the aftermath of an encounter with a tigress in India, remained pinned neatly to his lapel.

He turned to us as the door opened. "Good to see you, Mr. Holmes, at last. And Dr. Watson, of course."

Holmes nodded. "We shall learn what we can."

Gregson nodded towards the double doors that I well knew led to the examining room. "The medical examiner has been summoned, but has not yet arrived. Inside you will find the three perpetrators of the outrage."

"The three bodies," Holmes said.

The Commissioner caught the implications in Holmes's tone. "You do not think they are the perpetrators?"

"I will have no opinion until I have made observations."

The commissioner gave a glance at Gregson.

"We had thought there was sufficient evidence to indicate—" Gregson began, but Holmes was not listening. He had pushed through the double doors.

I followed him.

Three mortuary carts lay parallel to one another on the white-tiled floor, alongside the single mortuary slab. The electric light gleamed on the grey marble surface, and on the white porcelain of the laboratory sink behind the slab. The light also clearly illuminated the three bodies that lay fully clothed, each resting on a clean white sheet that draped down over the side of each cart. The woman's body lay between the bodies of the two men. Mercifully, white towels shrouded the three faces.

"Do we have identification papers?" Holmes asked.

"None of any sort," Gregson said. "No letters, no wallets on the men, no coin-purse on the woman. Apparently, they all wished to remain anonymous."

"Or their employer did," the Commissioner said.

"Then let us begin with the clothes," Holmes said, directing his attention to one body after another as he spoke. "They are all dusty and torn, as might be expected under the circumstances. But of good quality, woollen, with a heavy weave, though frayed around the sleeves and elbows. The woman's jacket and skirt are grey tweed, also with signs of long usage. Her stockings are cotton, dyed black."

He looked quickly inside the coat lapels, and the collars. "The labels have been removed."

"Again, anonymous," Gregson said.

"Now, the woman's boots," Holmes continued, ignoring the remark. "Dusty and scuffed. Well-worn." He removed one. "There is no label. But the stitch-work in the sole is recent. And the construction is sturdy and practical, rather than the ornamental fashion one would expect from a London boot maker."

Gregson said, "The hands are what I particularly noticed. The marks on the fingers."

"Very well, the fingers are not calloused or stained, indicating that none of these three was accustomed to heavy work or picking oakum in prison. However, the pallor one would expect to see on the wrists and palms is tinged with blue."

"I saw no marks of strangulation on their necks," said Gregson.

Holmes lifted three towels, one after another, exposing chins but not faces. "Nor do I."

"The medical examiner will determine the cause of death," I put in.

Holmes nodded. "Quite correct, and we are pressed for time. Moving on, I do see dirt smudges on several fingertips of both men. Also, there are scorch marks on the thumb and forefinger of the woman's right hand."

"Correct," said Gregson, with a nod to the Commissioner.

"From this you concluded," Holmes went on, "that the two men hefted the manhole cover, and that the woman threaded a fuse through the hole in the manhole cover, dropped the bomb inside and then, holding the fuse between her right thumb and forefinger, struck a match to it."

"Yes," said Gregson.

"Which would imply that the woman mishandled either the match or the fuse."

"Or that the fuse burned too rapidly."

Holmes turned to me. "Dr. Watson. Would you kindly examine the woman's right forefinger and thumb."

I did so.

Realisation immediately struck me, and I drew in my breath. "The woman's finger and thumb are indeed charred," I said, "but there is no swelling or blistering."

"What do you make of that?" asked the Commissioner.

Holmes held up his hand. "First, Dr. Watson, would you examine the knees of the woman? They are visible where her stockings have been torn."

"There are abrasions on both the knees," I said. "There is grit, likely from the road, ground into the abrasions. But, again, there is no swelling. Nor is there any bruising."

Holmes nodded. "Now, Doctor, would you please give us your medical conclusion derived from these two observations?"

"The medical conclusion is obvious. When the injuries to her hand and knees were sustained, the woman was dead."

"Thank you, Dr. Watson." Holmes turned to Gregson and the Commissioner. "I would expect the medical examiner will draw similar conclusions from an examination of the other two bodies."

"So, these three did not do the bombing," said the Commissioner.

"But how did they come to be on the scene at the time of the explosion?" asked Gregson. "And who lit the fuse?"

"There was no fuse. Whoever planted the bomb did so earlier, likely before dawn, under cover of darkness, and arranged matters to implicate the three victims. The perpetrator made the appropriate marks on the manhole cover. The bomb would have been detonated by a clockwork timing device, rather than a fuse. The three unfortunates we see here were killed elsewhere and then brought to Whitehall, likely in a van, or a coach with a rear luggage rack and a tarp to hold the bodies. The vehicle waited on the roadside until the appointed hour. Then, when the bomb had detonated and all bystanders were fleeing or staring at the manhole cover or the smoke, the vehicle drove off, dropping the bodies behind it."

"Which explains why the bodies were found with their arms outstretched," said Gregson.

"Indeed. I recommend you canvass local companies that rent vehicles and ask if any are missing. The perpetrators would likely pay cash and use a false name. Now, Dr. Watson and I must leave you. We have urgent business at Baker Street."

"Don't you want to examine the faces?" asked Gregson.

"I should like photographs, of course. But the examination and the cause of death are the province of the medical examiner. I should, of course, appreciate seeing the full report, particularly anything that might help us identify the three victims, whose identities someone has taken pains to conceal."

"Anything else?"

Holmes paused. For a long moment, he appeared lost in thought.

Then he clapped his palm to his forehead and said, "I have been a fool, and a lazy one at that!" He dropped to his hands and knees, his head oscillating back and forth, scanning the four corners of the room.

"Watson," he said, "the laboratory sink. Turn on the water faucet and plug the drain. Now!"

The intensity of his tone brooked no questions or hesitation. I acted immediately.

When the water was running, I saw him kneeling beside the centre cart.

Twisting his body, he reached under the sheet that hung down from the edge of the cart and very slowly pulled out an object the size of a small bread loaf, covered in a white towel. Holding it at arm's length, away from me, he stood and backed slowly and carefully in my direction.

"Now, step aside," he said.

He dropped the towel on the floor and deposited the object into the sink. When he moved away, I heard a metallic ticking, and saw, shimmering beneath the still-running water, a clockwork mechanism. Its wheels were moving.

Insulated wires connected it to two brown tubes, each the size of a cigar.

The three of us stared at Holmes.

He reached into the water and did something to the mechanism. The wheels stopped.

"A dynamite bomb with a timer," Gregson said, his voice chalky with relief.

"The same type must have been used to destroy the water main in Whitehall," said Commissioner Bradford. "Proves your theory, Mr. Holmes."

"I should post police guards at this location for as long as the bodies remain here," Holmes said. "Inspector Gregson, you should also have your men search the premises for the body of the hospital janitor."

CHAPTER 19: VIOLET

Violet sat by the sitting room fireplace in 221B Baker Street, trying not to shiver. There was no actual fire burning in the hearth. That would have been an absurd request to make in the middle of July. But despite the fact that Violet had been able to change into dry clothes—Lucy had lent her a skirt and blouse from the spare wardrobe she kept downstairs in 221A—she felt as chilled as though crystals of ice were forming inside her veins.

Mr. Holmes was speaking, and Violet realised with a jolt that he was addressing her.

"Can you tell us everything that you either heard or observed during your interlude with Mr. Blinder and Urquhart?"

Violet cleared her throat, making an effort to pull herself together. An hour or so ago, she had been absolutely certain that she was going to suffer an extremely unpleasant death. But she hadn't. As humbling as it was to owe her life to a child, Violet knew that the boy Flynn had saved her.

He and Becky were currently downstairs in the kitchen, where Flynn's clothes could dry off in front of the cook stove. Unlike Becky, Flynn didn't have spare clothes of his own and had categorically refused to borrow any.

Mr. Holmes stood near the bay window, Lucy and her husband Jack were sitting together on the sofa, and Dr. Watson was at the tea table, seated across from Preston.

The fact that Preston was also present for this meeting wasn't improving Violet's poise or her ability to concentrate.

Preston was leaning back in his chair with his long legs stretched out in front of him. He wore his usual broken-in boots, corduroy jacket and string tie with the long-horn cow's-head fastener. He looked as out of place here as a covered wagon being driven down the avenues of Windsor Palace.

If you judged strictly on appearances, he ought to be roping cows or strumming a guitar in front of an open campfire. And yet Violet knew he was listening, analysing, and meticulously cataloging every word that was spoken.

He raised a hand now. "Sorry to interrupt, Mr. Holmes. But it might be useful if Miss Leverton began at the beginning, so to speak, and started from when she left Baker Street this morning."

He met Violet's gaze with a bland look.

Violet just barely stopped herself from coming back with the snappish reply, *Before I foolishly went off on my own, do you mean?*

Whether or not Preston was trying to underscore her stupidity, she had made the mistake of travelling in the direction of the Junior Carlton Club without telling anyone where she was going or what her plans were—largely because she'd been goaded by Preston's air of all-knowing superiority.

Stupid she might be, but she could at least try to avoid making the same mistake twice.

"There's not very much to tell," she said evenly. "But you're welcome to the facts. I thought it likely that Calloway might have mailed the stolen bonds to the Junior Carlton Club. Unfortunately, Urquhart and Blinder had the same idea. They kidnapped me off the street and drugged me with chloroform or ether. When I came to—" she stopped, but went on without letting her voice waver. "When I came fully back to consciousness, I was on the boat that eventually sank."

She snapped off the memory of the axe and the blood and the icy rising water lapping at her mouth and nose, then went on in the same dispassionate tone.

"I'm afraid Urquhart and Blinder didn't tell me anything useful about their future plans. They were waiting for someone—a messenger, I think, who was coming to tell them whether the bonds really were at the Junior Carlton Club."

Mr. Holmes nodded. "Becky saw him there. Patterson was his name. Unfortunately for him, once he had secured the bonds, his usefulness to Blinder was at an end."

Violet blinked away another memory, this time the image of Patterson's shocked face and sightlessly staring eyes.

"There was one thing," she said. "Just before Patterson arrived on board the ship, I overheard Blinder and Urquhart talking together. I didn't catch much of what they were saying, but I did overhear Blinder say something about a lock."

"A lock?" Holmes's brows drew together.

"Yes." Violet cast her mind back, trying to recall the exact words. "He said … yes, he was talking to Urquhart, and he said, First, I want results from the lock."

"Nothing more?" Mr. Holmes was still frowning.

"No. Because Patterson arrived then. He handed over an envelope—I assume it had the stolen bonds inside—and then Urquhart killed him."

"Quite so," Mr. Holmes said. He didn't look disappointed or judgmental. None of the others in the room did. But a nasty sense of failure slithered across Violet's skin all the same.

She'd been in the presence of both Urquhart and Blinder—had

actually spoken to both of them—and had managed to learn practically nothing beyond what they already knew.

"What happens now?" she asked.

Mr. Holmes gaze rested on her thoughtfully for a moment. "Now, Urquhart and Blinder believe that you are dead. And I think that for your own safety as well as the success of our venture, it would be as well if in the eyes of the world you were to remain deceased." He focused on her. "Will that cause any problems for you? Have you for example any relatives to whom you would wish to send private reassurance that you are in fact alive?"

"I—" Violet stopped, then shook her head.

There weren't. She had never really stopped to consider it before, but she was very much alone in the world. Her parents were both dead. The great aunt who'd taken her in after her mother died had long since passed away. Her grandfather had died years before her mother and father's murders.

She didn't even have any close friends. She was on perfectly pleasant speaking terms with some of her neighbours back in Chicago. But would any of them feel more than a brief pang of regret—if that—if they heard that she had been killed in a boating accident?

"No, there's no one," Violet said.

"Excellent." Mr. Holmes spoke without apparent irony. From his point of view, it probably was all to the good that she had no close relationships in her life. "In that case, I propose that we give your name to the newspapers along with Mr. Patterson's, to be reported as having drowned in the unfortunate accident on the Thames today, wherein a steam ship's engine exploded and carried the vessel to the river bottom. Urquhart and Blinder will believe that they put you successfully out of the way, thus leaving no witnesses who can provide so much as a clue to where they may have gone."

Preston set the cup of coffee he'd been drinking back on the table. "Seems like we don't have much in the way of clues in any case," he said.

"I'm so sorry," Violet said. This time she didn't quite manage to suppress her temper. "Next time someone is attempting to murder me, I'll be sure to make him stop and fill out a detailed questionnaire as to his future plans."

Preston held up his hands. "No offense intended. I just meant that as far as I can see, it'll be hard to get a line on either Blinder or Urquhart, given how motivated they probably are to stay out of sight."

"There was one other thing," Violet said. The tiny detail had just popped into her head when she'd looked at Preston. "He mentioned your sister."

The moment she heard the words leave her mouth, she regretted them.

Preston's expression didn't overtly change, and yet his face hardened, somehow, his blue gaze taking on the sheen of polished metal.

When he said nothing, Mr. Holmes said, mildly, "Your sister, Mr. Preston?"

For once, Violet had no difficulty whatsoever in guessing at Preston's thoughts. With every fibre of his being he was hating that the subject of his sister had come up. And what was more, he probably thought that she'd done it deliberately, as payback for his criticism.

Had she intended it that way? She'd spoken without thinking, but she honestly didn't think she had.

Surely even she wouldn't have been that petty.

The hardening of Preston's expression lasted only a moment, then he turned to Mr. Holmes with his usual easy unconcern, crossing one booted ankle over the other. "My sister Pauline was a factory worker at Silverman's, a competitor of Mr. Blinder's. She and a lot of the other workers there fell ill. Poisoned, it turned out."

"Poisoned." Mr. Holmes's brows edged upwards a fraction of an inch. "I see. That is quite interesting."

"You could say that. Blinder was the one who'd done it, but we could never prove it."

Preston didn't look at Violet as he said it, but she wondered whether he was recalling their final meeting with Mr. Pinkerton, too.

Because fate hadn't apparently played Violet enough nasty pranks in her thirty-odd years of life, Mr. Pinkerton had decided to call Preston in to witness her being humiliated and fired from the Pinkerton's agency.

Well, to be fair, what Mr. Pinkerton had actually wanted was to demand whether Preston had put her up to investigating Blinder. But the effect was the same.

Preston had looked at her for a long moment, then finally opened his mouth to answer ...

Even now, Violet still had absolutely no idea what he might have said. But she hadn't given him the chance.

She'd fisted her hands and spoken over him, looking directly at Mr. Pinkerton.

Mr. Preston had nothing to do with my decision. I have been and am working completely alone.

Preston had avoided her after that, which was absolutely fine by Violet. Except that now here she and Preston were, working another case from opposite ends.

Score another point for fate's nasty sense of humour.

"What did Blinder say about Pauline?" Preston asked her now.

"Nothing, really." Violet swallowed, forcing herself to speak matter-of-factly. "Just that you had a good deal to worry about in caring for her."

"At any rate," Mr. Holmes said, speaking into the uncomfortable silence that followed, "Police security will now be increased at the water stations. The patrolmen will be advised to keep watch over manholes, as well."

"Manholes?" Violet made yet another effort to gather her wits. "Why?"

"Because our friends Urquhart and Blinder have been occupying themselves with more than stolen bonds," Mr. Holmes said. "We believe they were responsible for an explosion that destroyed the Whitehall water main."

"The water main?" Violet repeated. "Why would they have done such a thing?"

Dr. Watson had been quiet, but now spoke. "We believe it to be an attempt to undermine the current government. A breakdown of the water system in an area as important as Whitehall will inevitably suggest to the public that the London water system is neglected and dangerously in need of repair—particularly if the newspaper reporters get hold of the story, which we all know that they will. The papers will whip everyone up into a frenzy of outrage over the lack of clean drinking water, and the public will believe that the government is neglecting its responsibilities to its own citizens here at home in order to fund a reckless war with the Boers in faraway South Africa."

Preston looked across the table at Dr. Watson. His expression was as hard to read as ever, but Violet had some practice in deciphering Preston's inscrutable, lazy-eyed calm, and thought that he now appeared to have been struck by a new and sudden idea.

"So, we're thinking that Blinder and Urquhart are in the pay of the Germans, then?"

"The Germans would certainly have an interest in seeing our troops in South Africa withdrawn," Lucy said. "England's loss of international prestige would be Germany's gain."

"Not to mention the enormous deposits of gold and diamonds that are at stake," Mr. Holmes said. "To return, though, to the matter at hand, the police will be searching for Urquhart and Blinder. However, I do not hold out much hope for their immediate capture. After departing from the launch that carried them away from the sinking vessel today, they could be practically anywhere."

Lucy's husband Jack had also been listening in silence. Tall, dark, and broad-shouldered, he had been introduced to Violet as a sergeant at Scotland Yard, and she thought he had the air of tightly coiled, watchful energy that most policemen she knew acquired.

Preston had the same sense of electric readiness; he just concealed it extremely well.

Jack now straightened and spoke for the first time, addressing Mr. Holmes. "The three bodies that were found at the scene of the bombing—the ones who were supposed to look as though they'd been responsible—how were they dressed?"

"Heavy woollen tweeds and sturdy, practical boots, all three."

Jack nodded, as though that had been the answer he was expecting. "Not Londoners in July."

"It would appear unlikely," Mr. Holmes said.

Lucy turned to her husband, her expression one of dawning realisation. "You're thinking about the name? Urquhart?"

Jack nodded. "That, and the words Miss Leverton overheard Blinder use. 'Results from the lock.'"

Mr. Holmes was leaning up against the window with half-lowered lids and a blank expression, which Violet interpreted to mean the same thing it did when Preston's face took on that same look: keen interest and furious thinking, masked by indifference.

"It would fit," Mr. Holmes said.

"What would fit, Holmes?" Dr. Watson interrupted with an air of long-suffering patience. "For those of us not adept at mind reading, could you explain what the three of you"—his gesture encompassed Lucy, Jack, and Mr. Holmes—"are talking about?"

"Urquhart Castle," Lucy answered. "It's a ruined castle in Scotland." She looked at her husband. "I once performed *The Mikado* not far from there, when I was with the D'Oyly Carte company. That's how I've heard of the place. But how did you know about it?"

"The Yard. Inspector Lestrade got a call from the local constabulary a month or two back. There'd been reports of a strange creature being sighted in the water there. The locals were terrified. Apparently, there are legends about the same creature going back centuries, and the recent sightings had stirred it all up again. The police were hoping that by calling in Scotland Yard, they could put the matter to rest for good."

"Inspector Lestrade was asked to investigate a sea monster?" Lucy's lips were twitching, her green eyes bright with amusement. "I wish I could have been there to see his reaction. Or maybe I don't. I'm not sure the reality could live up to what I'm imagining."

Jack grinned, which made him look less hard-edged and intimidating. "Lestrade nearly burst a blood vessel when the telegram from Scotland came through. Had a lot to say about wasting valuable police time with ignorant superstition."

Dr. Watson interrupted again, still speaking patiently. "As amusing as that may be, I'm afraid that the rest of us still have no idea what you're talking about."

Violet did actually know. She should have realised it sooner—possibly even while she was on board the doomed boat, given that she was the one who'd done the most research into Urquhart's family history and background. But if she'd been slow to see the connections, she at least now fully shared the realisation that had struck both Lucy and Jack.

She kept silent, though, letting Lucy be the one to answer.

"If we're right," Lucy said, "Blinder wasn't talking about a lock in the sense of our English word. What Violet overheard was the Scottish word: Loch. We think that Blinder and Urquhart may be travelling to Loch Ness."

CHAPTER 20: VIOLET

"Loch Ness." Dr. Watson appeared to be taking that in. "I see. So you believe, Holmes, that the bodies found at the scene of the bombing had actually been brought here from Scotland?"

"Their apparel would indicate that probability. The final autopsy report will no doubt help to determine whether they were killed in Scotland and brought here, or kidnapped and brought to London before being killed. But bringing in three victims from out of town to take the blame for the bombing has, if I am right, a dual advantage: one, it would take the police longer to identify the bodies, since in the ordinary course of things, they would begin with missing persons reports from here in London. And two, any officers of the law looking into the case of persons who went missing in Scotland would be unlikely to search in London until it was too late."

"You believe that Urquhart and Blinder had some motive for getting those three people in particular out of the way?" Lucy asked.

"Indeed." Mr. Holmes put the tips of his fingers together, resting his index fingers against his upper lip. "Everything about this operation indicates careful planning and a high degree of organization."

"So much is clear from the bomb we found planted in the hospital mortuary," Dr. Watson said.

"Bomb?" Lucy looked up quickly. "You didn't mention that part."

Holmes made a dismissive gesture. "A fairly simple affair, easily disarmed."

He sounded as though he disarmed bombs on a regular basis. Which for all Violet knew, he very well might.

"Nonetheless," Lucy continued, "they must have anticipated that you would wish to examine the bodies in person, so they infiltrated the hospital in the guise of the janitor and planted the bomb in advance of your visit there."

"Possibly." Holmes still sounded as though he were discussing the weather rather than an attempt at murder. "But the bomb might have been merely an attempt to destroy the evidence presented by the bodies, rather than a targeted attack on Watson and myself. The more pertinent issue is the question of identifying the three victims. As Lucy suggested, I would hypothesize that the three bodies found in Whitehall today were individuals who had got in the way of whatever operations Urquhart and Blinder are carrying out in Scotland, and who had thus made themselves a liability that had to be eliminated."

"But what might those operations be, Holmes?" Dr. Watson's brows were drawn together. "What possible interest could Urquhart and Blinder have in a remote Loch in the Scottish Highlands?"

"The better question is how those interests relate to the bombing of the Whitehall water main," Mr. Holmes said. "For the moment, we have enough data to theorise, but no more."

Dr. Watson's expression suggested that he didn't even have enough data to formulate a theory, but he kept silent.

Preston spoke. He was still leaning back casually, his booted ankles crossed. But Violet knew he'd been taking in every word.

"How certain are we that it was Loch Ness the two of them

meant? So far as I've heard, Scotland's got more lochs than holes in a piece of Swiss cheese. You've got the possible connection to Urquhart castle, but how common a name is Urquhart in those parts? Do we know that there's actually any connection there?"

"There is." Violet had a second to wonder whether Preston knew this as well as she did, and had only asked the question to gauge how extensive her own research had been. But she went on, "Urquhart was actually born there. His parents owned a very successful pharmacy business in the nearest city, the port of Inverness."

"That is extremely useful information, Miss Leverton." Holmes nodded approval.

"Thank you." Violet heard how stiff and cold the words sounded, but she couldn't seem to inject any more warmth into her tone.

She'd never had time to be lonely before. If anything, she'd revelled in her independence, her ability to solve a case and send a criminal to jail entirely through her own, unaided efforts. She worked alone, and that was the way she liked it.

But now, looking around the room, she could see what a close-knit team they all were.

Of everyone in the room, only Lucy and Mr. Holmes were related by actual ties of blood, and yet all of them—Dr. Watson, Lucy, Jack, even the two children downstairs—were obviously a family.

Lucy and Jack were one of those rare married couples who didn't only love each other, but genuinely liked each other, as well. They weren't even sitting particularly close together on the couch, and they certainly weren't being romantic. Yet their happiness was clear in every word they spoke, every gesture they made.

The others all finished each other's sentences and anticipated one another's thoughts in the way that family did.

And here she sat, an outsider who didn't belong here, maybe didn't even belong anywhere, not really.

The thought brought a twinge of an uncomfortably dry, hollow achy feeling.

"We still don't know for certain that Urquhart and Blinder will head up to Scotland, though," Preston said. "Blinder said he wanted to wait until they got results from the Loch. He didn't say anything about visiting the place in person."

"Very true," Mr. Holmes agreed. "Which is why I propose that we divide our forces. Watson, Jack, and I will remain here in London to follow up on the investigation of the bombing and pursue any leads as to Blinder's contacts here in the city."

"And you want me to travel up to Inverness?" Lucy asked.

"If you are willing."

"Of course. I can bring Flynn and Becky along with me," Lucy said.

"You're going to bring the children?" Whether she belonged here or not, Violet was startled enough to interrupt the discussion.

"Oh yes." Lucy's expression was a blend of amusement and resignation. "If I didn't, they'd only try to box themselves up in a freight container and mail themselves to Scotland, or do something even more hair-raising. You can play the part of their governess, if you'd like," she added.

"What?" Violet was so startled that for a moment she wondered whether she'd heard correctly. "You want me to join you?"

"Of course." Lucy looked mildly surprised. "You're already familiar with both Blinder's and Urquhart's backgrounds—and you've met them in person, which is more than I've done. You're far more likely to be able to anticipate what actions they might take. Unless you don't want to be involved in the investigation anymore?" Lucy's gaze turned gentler, and yet at the same time wasn't at all judgmental or pitying. She spoke completely matter-of-factly. "No one here would blame you if you wanted to take some time to recover after what you've been through today."

"I'm fine." Despite the warmth of Lucy's manner, Violet's voice still sounded stiff in her own ears.

It wasn't Lucy's fault, but she was one of those women who always made Violet feel thoroughly inadequate. Beautiful, intelligent, successful, and loved by everyone, everywhere she went.

Violet could practically feel herself being tugged back through time, transforming into the shy, awkward schoolgirl who'd been mercilessly bullied by the other girls for her awful clothes and her father's reputation as a worthless drunk.

"I'm quite ready to come," she said firmly. There was also no chance that she was going to admit to any sort of weakness with Preston here, looking on. "Although I don't think I'm especially well qualified to act as a governess."

Lucy look of amusement deepened. "That's all right. I can guarantee that you won't be any less qualified to be a governess than Flynn and Becky are to have one."

"It's decided, then," Mr. Holmes said. "The four of you can be on the train to Inverness tomorrow. And you, Mr. Preston? Have you decided what course of inquiry you would prefer to pursue?"

"Well, now." Preston looked back at Mr. Holmes, although Violet thought his gaze flicked just briefly to her before he said, "I'm not entirely certain yet. I've got a couple of irons in the fire, but nothing definite. Let me think about it and get back to you."

Chapter 21: Flynn

Flynn came awake only three hours after he'd gone to bed. The time was 3:45 AM, according to the clock on his hotel room dresser. The heavy drapes were drawn, but he could see faint sunlight where the two woollen panels came together. He was in Scotland, a day's journey north, and Mr. Holmes had told him the sunrise would be earlier than it was in London.

He rolled out of bed and stretched himself the way he always did. Then he put on his trousers and socks and shoes, parted the drapes, opened the window, and climbed out onto the fire escape.

The air of Inverness was cool and clear, except for the mist coming in from the sea. Very different from the heat in London, or on the stuffy train they'd taken to get here.

He stood a few moments, getting his bearings, trying to match what he saw with what he remembered from the map he'd studied on the train. Directly across, the River Ness and Inverness Harbour lay four stories below him, shadowy in the light of the sunrise. To his left, the dark silhouettes of a castle and church spires rose up to dominate the horizon. To his right was a wide green expanse that reminded him of the Regents Park in London, only without buildings. From his high vantage point, it looked relatively small.

He would head for the churches first, and then the park, he decided.

He'd agreed with Mr. Holmes to play the part of a young toff, wearing the uncomfortable clothes and stiff boots that remained in the wardrobe in his room. He planned to put those on when he came back to meet Becky, Lucy and Miss Violet for breakfast at seven-thirty.

But before that, he wanted to accomplish something on his own.

Clambering down the fire escape ladder, taking care not to make noise, he reached the end, ten feet above a garden border with bushes and concrete planters that ran alongside this section of the hotel.

No one was watching, so he gripped the last rung and slid his legs out over the edge. Then he twisted around, dangled for a moment, and dropped.

He made no sound on the garden mulch. A minute later he was strolling quickly towards the street that he knew had several churches nearby. Churches were good for what he had in mind, because vicars weren't too strict about people down on their luck and sleeping rough in the churchyard.

But he went by three churches without success. He saw several sleepers, but all of them seemed too old. He needed someone of his own age.

After the third try, he headed south towards the big green field. There, he thought, people would also be likely to sleep, just as they did in the London parks.

The sun was up by the time he got there, and the dew sparkled on the grass. He headed for the centre of the field, where he saw a shadowy shape curled up at the base of wooden bleachers about twenty feet wide and five rows high. The field, Flynn knew, was where Inverness athletes came to compete. A side benefit of coming here at this hour was to scope out the place, which might attract some crowds, and therefore be a spot for the kind of public catastrophe Mr. Holmes had talked about yesterday.

But for now, the objective was to see if this huddled sleeper would do. In an unfamiliar city, if he was to help Mr. Holmes the way he wanted, Flynn needed a connection of some sort. Someone who knew the ins and outs of Inverness the way Flynn and his cronies knew London. In other words, an Irregular of his own. He grinned at the thought.

The kid was maybe a couple years younger than Flynn. He was curled up but with his head twisted upward, so Flynn could see his stringy black hair partially covering his pale forehead and one of his high-boned cheeks.

It looked promising.

Then Flynn saw the crutch. Rags cushioned a crosspiece atop a battered, dirty bare-wood pole.

So. Considering that Irregulars had to go everywhere and not be noticed anywhere, maybe this kid wasn't so promising after all.

Flynn was on the point of turning away when the kid sat up and saw him.

"Hey," the kid said.

Flynn nodded. Spread his hands open in the time-honoured gesture of peace.

"Whit ye want?" the kid asked.

"Mind if I sit?"

The kid shrugged. Flynn sat. He decided to follow the approach he'd worked out.

He pointed towards where he'd come, to the outline of a castle on the horizon.

"Is that Urquhart's Castle?" He pronounced it 'Urkut', the way he'd heard Mr. Holmes say it yesterday.

"D'ye have any money?" the kid replied.

"Maybe."

"Then maybe I tell ye."

Flynn had some money from Mr. Holmes. He took out a shilling from his pocket and showed it to the boy.

"What's your name?"

"Kevin," the boy said. "Yours?"

"Flynn." He pointed to the silhouette of the castle on the horizon. "Now, Kevin, do you want to tell me what that is?"

Kevin plucked the shilling from Flynn's palm and tucked it away. "'At's the Duke's Castle."

"Where's Urquhart's, then?"

"Not far. Want me to take you there?"

Flynn gestured at the crutch. "Can you?"

Kevin got to his feet. To Flynn's surprise, he bent over and hefted the crutch in one hand. Then he grinned. "This is just for show. And if I need to crack somebody's 'ead."

"Show?"

Kevin twisted his foot inwards, wincing convincingly. "See? I wait till there's a pretty good crowd in the stands. I hobble over where the runners are doing their exercise things. I try to copy an' I fall over sometimes. Then I hobble back past the stands and sit, wi' me cap in my lap. People see me an' put brass in 'cause they feel sorry." He pulled a dirty cloth cap from his coat and dangled it with a pained expression and imploring eyes. "Right pitiful, ye ken?"

Flynn gave a nod, half admiring the illusion and half wondering if the boy could be trusted.

Oh, well. The lad had talent.

"Take me there, then," he said, accompanying the words with another shilling.

The two set out, walking briskly. Kevin carried his crutch under his arm, his coat draped over it. They were headed back to town, in the direction of Flynn's hotel. Not more than a minute later, they were on the high street, with shops on either side. Ordinary buildings. Two stories tall, no more.

No castle.

"Here we are, then Mr. Flynn. This is Urquhart's."

The building was dirty brick, at the end of the block. Brick. The sign above the front door read "Urquhart's Herbals. Nostrums and Tonics." Flynn guessed the Scots spelled their words differently.

"This isn't a castle."

"Never said it was. But it's Urquhart's, all the same."

A thought tugged at Flynn's memory. Miss Violet had said Urquhart had been a chemist. "Ever seen the bloke who owns the place?"

"Maybe. Wot's 'e look like?"

Flynn remembered, from when he'd been hiding in the river bank bushes. "Oily. Face like a weasel. But yellow. Pasty yellow-like and dirty."

"Where do you know him from?"

"Whitechapel."

"Wot's that?"

"In London," Flynn said.

"Where you're from, eh?"

Flynn nodded.

"That's why you don't talk proper."

"What about this Urquhart? You seen him?"

"Why do you want to know?"

"That castle," Flynn said. Suddenly he had a bad feeling about the way the conversation was going. "I heard of a place called Urquhart's Castle. My aunt wants to see it. Maybe the man Urquhart knows how to get in, him being the same name and all."

Kevin pointed to the sign on the door. It read: Hours M-F, 9-6 "Why don't you stay around till nine and ask yourself?"

"Can't."

"I'll stay and ask then. For another shilling, of course. Where are you staying?"

Flynn said, "Here and there. Like you."

"Where's your aunt, then?"

Flynn kept a straight face. "She comes in on the train this afternoon."

"Tell you what. I'll meet you at those bleachers back there. Noon."

"Noon, then," Flynn said. He turned to leave.

"Have my shilling ready."

Flynn walked away, thinking that at least he'd have something to report when he met Lucy and the others for breakfast.

Chapter 22: Becky

"An egg and spoon race?" Becky's lip curled.

Flynn shrugged. "It's the only one you're eligible to enter. See?" He showed her the printed program that he'd been studying. "100-yard race for girls under 14. Egg and spoon. It'll give you a chance to talk to people—especially the kids from around here. Find out whether they've seen or heard anything helpful."

Lucy and Violet had talked everything over this morning while they had sausages and oatmeal for breakfast at the Inn. They were going to look around Inverness, making inquiries about the three dead bodies that had been found at the site of the Whitehall bombing, while Becky and Flynn looked around the Scottish Games.

Children often were the best place to start when it came to hunting for leads in a case. Becky knew that. They usually knew more than the adults did, because they could look and listen without anyone noticing them.

Still, Becky protested, "Why can't you enter the lemonade and biscuit race? The program says that's for boys under fourteen."

They were standing on the edge of the Dornach Highland Games grounds, a large grassy park, ringed by trees. The castle and church spires rose up tall against the skyline in the town beyond.

Tents had been set up all around the field for the various events, and hundreds of people were milling around. Massive-looking men in kilts hefted wooden poles as big as trees for what they called the caber toss. Women in tartan plaid skirts and long woollen stockings were practicing sword dances, hopping nimbly back and forth across blades crossed on the ground. The keening, wailing music of bagpipes filled the air, along with the voices of the crowds.

"Because first of all, I don't even know what a biscuit and lemonade race is," Flynn said. "And second, because that's for locals only. See?"

He pointed to the top line on the program.

"I'm not a local either."

"But you can do a convincing Scottish accent, after all the lessons Lucy gave you on the train. No one's going to take me for Scottish."

That was true. Flynn was an expert pickpocket and sneak thief, but he wasn't very good at acting, much less putting on a false accent.

"And third, because I've got to keep an eye out for Kevin," Flynn said.

Becky looked up quickly. "Kevin? Who's that?"

"A street kid I met here. Promised to watch Urquhart's chemist's shop for me and let me know if Urquhart himself showed his face."

So Flynn had found a local informant. That was just like him. "Do you trust this Kevin?" Becky asked.

Flynn snorted, as though that were such a ridiculous question, he couldn't even imagine asking it. "Of course not. But he wants the shilling I promised him, which means I've got to hang around those bleachers"—he waved a hand at the wooden bleachers set up for spectators—"until he comes."

Becky blew out a breath. "Fine. I'll enter the egg and spoon race. But if I catch you laughing, I warn you, I'm going to throw my egg right in your face."

* * *

Becky clutched her spoon, trying to keep her egg—which seemed to have a mind of its own—from hopping off and onto the ground.

She was lined up on the starting line with all the other girls who'd entered, waiting for the referee—or whatever you called the official in an egg and spoon race—to blow his whistle and start them off.

The wait seemed to be taking forever. Apparently one girl claimed that another girl had stolen her spoon, and they were now huddled off on the sidelines with the pair of judges, who were having to listen to both girls' stories.

Although Becky wasn't exactly in a hurry. She wasn't sure she was going to take a single step without smashing her egg.

Flynn had suggested she sneak into the tea tent and use one of the gas rings to hard-boil it, and right now she was wishing she'd taken his advice.

"I saw you over at the Inn." The child next to her—a fat, blond-haired girl of around eight, with teeth that stuck out over her lower lip—turned to give Becky an accusing stare. "You're not from here. You're a visitor."

Becky shut her eyes for a quick second. Wonderful. She hadn't had any trouble fooling the middle-aged woman in charge of the race into thinking she was a local. The woman had been surrounded by a swarm of girls all waving their entrance fees in her face and had barely given Becky a second glance.

She should have known that this couldn't be so easy.

She turned to the blond girl, widening her eyes into a look of earnest pleading. "Oh, please don't tell on me! I know I'm not a local girl, but as soon as I saw there was an egg and spoon race here, I couldn't help myself, I just had to enter."

"Really?" The other girl looked skeptical. Understandably.

"Oh yes!"

Over in the spectator's area, Becky could see Flynn struggling to keep a straight face, but she ignored him.

As long as she was stuck playing this role, she might as well do it fully. That was what Lucy always said about a theatrical performance: the key to convincing your audience was to commit to your part whole-heartedly.

"I've always wanted to enter an egg and spoon race—always! I don't think I'll win, though," she added sadly.

That much was true, anyway.

The blond girl studied her a second, eyes narrowed, then she apparently either decided to be charitable—or else that Becky wasn't enough competition to bother reporting her.

"My name's Moira," she said. "What's yours?"

"Becky. And I'm not just a visitor," Becky added. "My aunt Mary's second cousin's uncle has family here."

"Really?" Moira looked interested. "What's their name?"

"Urquhart. I heard they once had a castle nearby here."

"Och, aye." Moira nodded. "Urquhart Castle's just a ruin, now, but it was a grand place once. Your aunt's cousin's uncle was a relation of theirs, did you say?"

Drat it, was that what she had said? Becky should have worked out her story in advance.

"That's right. My aunt told me when we decided to visit here to be sure and look up any family that might still live here. She'd lost touch with them, you see."

"That's a shame. I don't think you'll find any of your relations living here, though," Moira said. "The only Urquharts I know of ran the pharmacy, but they died years ago. I've heard my parents speaking of it, what a pity it is that their son—he inherited the business from them—doesn't take more of an interest. But he left and never came back, just lets Mr. Brown the shop manager run things for him—and Mr. Brown's no more honest than he should be and probably skims from the profits, or so my mother says, because he charges twice what a tin of tooth powder ought to cost."

Becky ignored the price of tooth powder and focused on the interesting part of what Moira had just said. "So Mr. Urquhart—the Urquhart's son, I mean—hasn't ever come back? Not even to visit?"

Moira started to shake her head, but the referee chose that moment to blow a piercing blast on the whistle, starting the race.

All the girls stampeded off, balancing their eggs on the ends of their spoons. Becky followed, gripping the handle of her own spoon hard enough to leave imprints on her palm. Although she needn't have worried. She'd barely gone twenty yards before Moira tripped and went sprawling headlong.

"Are you all right?" Becky pocketed her egg so that she could crouch down beside the other girl.

Moira was crying and clutching her ankle, but she shook her head. "No, don't stop!" She swiped at her tears and tried to wave Becky away. "You'll be disqualified from the race if you stop for me!"

"It's all right." Egg and spoon races were more cutthroat than

Becky would have thought; none of the other girls spared Moira more than a passing glance. "Here, let me help you up."

Moira took her hand and tried to get to her feet, but she gave a sharp gasp and started crying again when she tried to put any weight on her injured ankle.

"Just lean on me." Becky put an arm around the other girl, and Moira, sniffing and hopping on her good leg, allowed herself to be helped off the field.

"I'm sorry!" Moira wailed. She scrubbed at her tears with the edge of her woollen sweater. "I'm always clumsy! And you said you'd always wanted to be in the egg and spoon race, and now I've gone and ruined it for you."

"Don't worry." Becky patted Moira's shoulder. Maybe she'd overdone the full commitment to her part a bit. "It … it turned out that it wasn't really as much fun as I thought it would be. Why don't we just sit down here." She helped Moira over to a patch of bare grass under the shade of a tree behind the bleachers. "You can tell me all the best places to visit around here. Is it really true that there's a monster in the Loch?"

"Och, that." Becky had chosen the right change of subject, because Moira's face instantly brightened. "Our teachers at school have always said it's just nonsense and superstition. But I've heard stories from people who've seen it with their own eyes! Why, just last month, Bobby Campbell was coming home from the pub late at night, and he swears he saw the creature rise up out of the water! A long neck like a snake's, he said it had, and a head like a dragon."

"Really?"

Moira nodded solemnly. "There's some say he was just drunk

at the time. But others have seen it, too! And—" Moira lowered her voice. "There's talk that the monster's dragging people into the water. To eat them!"

"Really?" Whether or not she believed that, it gave Becky the perfect chance to ask her next question. "Have people been going missing lately?"

"Maybe." Moira's voice sank to a hushed whisper. "My mother says—"

"Who's that you're talking to, Moira?" A sharp-featured woman in a grey dress and old-fashioned bonnet appeared over Moira's shoulder, giving Becky a suspicious look.

Moira turned. "Just a girl I met in the races, Mam. She's a visitor over at the Inn, and—"

Moira's mother didn't give her daughter a chance to finish. "Come away, Moira. It's high time we were leaving."

"But Mam, Becky helped me—"

"Come away, I said. What have I told you about talking to strangers?"

She didn't look at Becky as she said it. That wasn't so unusual. Plenty of adults treated children like pieces of furniture and didn't feel the least bit awkward talking about them as if they weren't even there.

But Moira's mother looked … tense, Becky thought. Her lips were pressed together into a thin line, and she was gripping her daughter's arm so hard that Moira winced.

She might just have been very strict and annoyed at Moira answering back. But Becky had had a good deal of practice at watching people's expressions, and right now she thought Moira's mother looked more frightened than angry.

"I'm sorry." Moira, still limping on her injured foot, cast an apologetic glance back over her shoulder as her mother hauled her away. "Maybe I'll see you about?"

Becky didn't even get the chance to answer before the crowds blocked her view of Moira and her mother.

"Anything useful?" Flynn asked.

Becky almost jumped at the sound of his voice, but covered it by turning around. Flynn was just stepping out from behind the tree where she and Moira had been sitting.

"You tell me. Didn't you hear everything we were talking about?"

"Nah, I only just got here," Flynn said. "Just as Mrs. Crabby was dragging the blonde kid away."

"Well, the blonde girl is Moira. I don't know her last name, she didn't tell me that. But she said that Urquhart left Scotland after his parents died and never came back. And the stories about the monster in the Loch are real, apparently. I mean, there really are stories about people having seen it recently, especially at night."

"How recent is recently?" Flynn asked.

"Last month? There may have been other sightings, too, but I didn't get the chance to ask any questions. The woman who dragged Moira off was her mother, and she didn't at all like Moira speaking to me."

"About the monster?"

Becky considered that. "Maybe. She probably did hear the last part of what Moira was telling me. She came up just as Moira was saying that other local people claim to have seen it besides the man she'd already mentioned. And that there are rumours that the monster is dragging people into the Loch and eating them. So, I asked her whether anyone from around here had gone missing lately. Because of the three bodies found at the site of the bombing in London. If they really were from this part of Scotland, someone would have to have noticed that they were gone. Moira said her mother knew something about it—"

"What?"

"I don't know. That's when her mother actually appeared and stopped her from saying anything else to me."

"Scared, you think?" Flynn asked.

Becky nodded slowly. The more she thought about it, the more she did think that Moira's mother had been frightened by something about their conversation.

"I don't know if she's frightened by the sea monster stories, or worried about Moira talking to me about them," she said. "Or whether she actually knows something about people who have gone missing."

Flynn scanned the crowd of people. "Think it's worth trying to find them again?"

Becky considered. "Maybe. If she was afraid of Moira talking to me, she's definitely not going to talk to either of us or answer questions. Besides, what about Kevin? Have you seen him yet?"

Flynn glanced back towards the bleachers, frowning. "No. Not a sign of him. And he should have been here by now."

"You think something's happened to him?"

"Maybe." Flynn's brows were still knitted together. "Or he found an easier way of earning a shilling."

Becky took a guess at what he was thinking. "Like going straight to Urquhart and telling him about us?"

"Maybe. If Urquhart's anywhere about, that is."

"Or Blinder."

"Or him," Flynn agreed.

Becky thought of the men they'd seen from a distance, the ones who'd grabbed Violet off the street. A shiver tried to slide down the length of her spine, but she ignored it. Being scared never helped anything, and finding Urquhart and Blinder was the entire reason that they had come to Scotland.

"In that case, maybe Moira and her mother actually are our best lead for now. I don't see finding them in this crowd." She gestured to the throngs of people all around them. "But I could speak to the woman in charge of the egg and spoon race. Pretend that Moira dropped a handkerchief or something that I want to give back, and ask whether she knows where Moira and her mother live. Not that Moira's mother is going to be any happier if we show up and knock on their door, but we could keep an eye on her—see where she goes and whether there's any sign that she's hiding something."

Flynn gave the bleachers one last frowning look, then nodded. "Sounds like our best plan."

CHAPTER 23: LUCY

Holmes always said that when looking for a missing person in a small town, the two places to begin were the pubs and the churches. Violet and I had decided to begin with the pubs, specifically an establishment on Academy Street on the edge of town closest to the River Ness.

A pleasant, cosy place called McGregor's, its bar room had a low ceiling with exposed timber beams and a big stone fireplace at one end.

Since it was early in the day, the place was deserted, save for an old man sitting at one end of the bar and looking as though he came here so often that he was practically part of the furniture.

Violet and I were questioning the pub owner, Mr. Owen McGregor. Or rather we were supposed to be. Violet kept turning to look out through the pub's small glazed windows.

"Your friend seems a wee bit nervous," Mr. McGregor said, nodding to her.

Violet had crossed to the pub door and was peering out into the street, where carts and carriages rattled past on their way to the Highland Games.

"She's just looking out for the friends whom we're supposed to meet here," I said.

"Friends, is it?"

Mr. McGregor was a big, phlegmatic looking man with

muscular arms and a fringe of brown hair combed down from a balding head. He had a square jaw, bulbous nose, and very shrewd-looking blue eyes, which at the moment were eyeing Violet.

He had the look I'd found was common in both policemen and men in his profession: the look that said he'd observed far too much of human nature to be surprised by anything anymore.

But he did look mildly curious. He was currently drying pint glasses with quick, deft twists of his towel and arranging them in a neat pyramid behind the bar. But his gaze remained on Violet.

"I've seen cats on hot bricks that were less jumpy-lookin.'"

That was unfortunately true. I'd had my doubts about Violet accompanying us on this trip, after what she'd lived through only the day before yesterday.

I'd stood in Violet's shoes almost exactly: drugged, kidnapped, and locked up by a ruthless enemy. I could remember all too clearly how long it had taken for me to feel safe again or to think with a clear head.

I'd said as much yesterday morning to Jack, before we'd left for the train station, and he'd smiled and asked what I would have done if anyone had tried to keep me out of an investigation on that account.

He had a point. I knew exactly what I would have done. I would have refused to be shut out, point-blank.

But that didn't stop me from worrying, not just that Violet was going to be more of a liability than a help on this trip, but that she was setting herself up for a very long and difficult road of recovery from what she'd endured.

My immediate concern at the moment, though, was that I was now going to need to change my approach to this conversation with Mr. McGregor. Well, maybe that had been inevitable. He seemed like a man who would probably have seen through any subterfuge or cover story in any case.

"We're private detectives," I said.

"Detectives, is it?" Mr. McGregor's eyebrows went up a notch, but that was apparently the extent of his capacity for registering shock. He studied me a moment, as though making up his mind whether or not I was being truthful, then nodded. "Aye, I see. I didna' think you had the look of summer visitors."

"We're authorised by the government to look into a recent bombing in London," I said.

"A bombing?" Mr. McGregor's eyebrows climbed slightly higher on his domed forehead this time. "And what's that got to do with us here?"

"We believe that the three victims of the bomb may have been from this area. Two men and one woman, all of them fairly young. Do you know of any reports of missing persons from around these parts?"

"Well, now." Mr. McGregor dried another glass with a twirl of his towel and considered. "That might be the Campbells. Two brothers and a sister. They've not been seen for weeks, now, though their mother says that there's naught to worry about."

"Who are the Campbells?" I asked.

"Their family ran the local whisky distillery. Old Rupert Campbell founded it, and his widow and children continued the business when he died. About three years back, that would have been. I used to carry their whisky here." He glanced over his shoulder at the various glass bottles ranged on shelves behind the bar. "Verra' good quality it was, too."

"But not anymore?"

"No, more's the pity." Mr. McGregor shook his head. "They'd several failed batches in a row, one after the other. I'd have liked to keep buying from them, to help out Mrs. Campbell, but what could I do?" He spread his hands. "I wouldna' be in business myself long if I tried to sell my customers an inferior product."

"Are they still in business?" Violet had been paying more attention to the conversation than I had thought, and now turned away from the doorway to ask the question.

"Oh, aye." Mr. McGregor nodded. "They're still running the distillery just down the road. Number 113, it is. Or rather, Widow Campbell is running it. As I say, no one's seen her children for weeks, though they used to be part of the operation. I dinna' know how their mother is still making a go of it."

CHAPTER 24: WATSON

"Now," said Commissioner Bradford. "What do we know, and how should we proceed?"

The Commissioner sat at the head of a long oak table familiar to both Holmes and me, in an upstairs book-lined conference room, one of a few in the Diogenes Club where talking was permitted. Holmes and I sat at the Commissioner's right. Across from us, both in uniform, were Tobias Gregson and Jack Kelly. Gregson had a stack of papers on the table before him. Preston was missing. I had thought he would attend, but we had not heard from him since our meeting at 221B Baker Street two days earlier.

Opposite the Commissioner, at the far end of the table, sat Mycroft Holmes.

The Commissioner beckoned to Gregson. "Inspector, you were in charge at the Whitehall explosion site. What do you suggest?"

"Well, sir, I'm thinking of the attempt at the mortuary to destroy the medical evidence."

The Commissioner grimaced.

"So, given that someone wanted to hide that evidence, I think it would be a good idea to start with the examiner's report on the three bodies."

He extracted several pages from his stack of papers. "I will read the salient points. First, death occurred at least two days prior to the Sunday when the bodies were found."

"More proof that they could not have detonated the bomb," said the Commissioner.

"Second, the lungs of all three victims were filled with fluid."

"Drowned?" the Commissioner asked.

"No, bodily fluid." Gregson squinted at the page. "Lymphatic fluid."

Holmes, who up until now had remained silent, resting his chin on his steepled fingertips, suddenly sat up. "Please continue, Inspector," he said.

"There were muscle tears indicating convulsions, particularly when taken with the distorted expressions of the faces."

"The cause of death?"

"Systemic organ failure. Throughout each of the three victims," he added.

"Marks on the bodies?"

"Other than the post-mortem injuries to the fingertips and knees, there were none."

"None, Inspector?" Holmes's tone had turned sharp.

"Sir?"

"At the mortuary, I observed a puncture behind the right ear of one of the men, and two comparable marks behind the left ears of the other two victims."

Gregson turned over the page. "Oh, yes. Quite. My apologies. My oversight. Here we are. 'Insect bites observed on the necks and chests of the victims. Fleas were observed when removing the clothes. Also, some marks may have been made by injection.'"

"Fleas?" The Commissioner appeared puzzled.

"The fleas would have done their work while the victims were confined," Holmes replied. "There would have been ample opportunity for injections while the victims were still alive."

"What would have been injected?" The Commissioner asked.

"A poison that causes massive organ failure, convulsions, pulmonary edema, and tinges the skin with the blue pallor that we all observed."

"But what poison is that?"

Holmes shrugged. "There are numerous tests that can be performed."

Gregson said, "The medical examiner has a paragraph on that in his report." He read:

"'Given the importance and urgency of the case, I conducted every test available to me for a toxic agent that would yield the conditions observed in the three bodies. Every test produced a negative result.'"

Holmes gave one of his tight little smiles.

"Why are you smiling, Sherlock?" Mycroft asked.

"Because the medical examiner has obligingly narrowed the field. We now must look for a deadly agent which remains unsusceptible to identification by any test."

"I fail to see how that offers us any advantage," said the Commissioner.

"Future events may clarify the situation," Holmes said. "For now, we can pursue two avenues of inquiry. First, to determine the identities of the victims, which may lead to a connection with the murderer. Second, to reason from the cause of the death of the victims. The toxic agent may be important not only in identifying the murderer, but also in identifying his future plans."

"You think a toxin may be connected with the Whitehall water main?" The Commissioner's face tightened with concern.

"Indeed."

"I have news in that regard," I said, "I was in Hyde Park this morning. I received this pamphlet from one of the soap-box orators."

I read:

"My fellow citizens, our hard-earned taxes are being systematically wasted on remote corners of the empire under the guise of patriotism. We have been made blind to a grave and horrific risk, right here at home. We have neglected our water purification systems, and now face the return of the deadly cholera epidemics that even now ravage India and less fortunate parts of the world. The blame must be laid at the feet of the current administration. They have shown poor judgment and blind ambition. We must vote them out, my friends. Vote them out!"

The memory of the speaker's furious oratory glowed vividly in my mind. I set the pamphlet down. "I asked the speaker his name. He gave it readily enough, claiming to be a paid actor hired for this specific assignment. He called it a performance."

"The very same argument appeared in a letter sent to the *Times* this morning," said Mycroft. "Of course, we shall see to it that it is not published. But other papers may not be so cooperative."

"Was there any mention of cholera in the medical examiner's report?" the Commissioner asked.

Gregson shook his head. "None, sir. But I'll have our men on the lookout for these pamphlets at Hyde Park. We will find out who's hiring these actors."

The Commissioner nodded his approval. There was a moment's silence.

Then Jack leaned forward.

"Lucy is in Inverness, looking for this Urquhart bloke," he said. "And I've been investigating the man named Blinder, who

Violet Leverton says orchestrated her kidnapping and also the theft of the bonds."

"What have you learned?"

"He has a fast yacht. It left Victoria Docks yesterday, bound for Dover. Harbour master says it gave no further destination when it passed through Dover into the Channel."

"You think it is bound for Inverness?" the Commissioner asked.

"Maybe. It was because of Blinder that we sent Lucy and Becky there—along with Flynn and Violet Leverton. Violet overheard Blinder say something to Urquhart that we thought connected to Inverness."

He broke off. "Admittedly it's all conjecture at this point. But what I suggest is that we have the Navy watch the sea lanes in the Channel and determine if Blinder's yacht is heading for Scotland. If it's headed for Inverness, we could have the Navy stop it."

"On what grounds?" the Commissioner asked.

"We're searching for stolen bonds, remember? And we have reason to believe they are on that yacht. We have the eyewitness evidence of Becky, who saw the bonds picked up by Blinder's courier, and of Flynn, who saw the courier deliver them to Blinder and Urquhart. And be murdered for his trouble."

Gregson added, "Delivered while the two were on a scow that they sunk with a bomb. The bomb used a timing device. As did the one used in Whitehall and the one used in the St. Thomas mortuary. Surely that's connection enough."

The Commissioner shook his head. "We have eyewitness evidence, yes, but identifying the two men who received delivery of the bonds … I fear we are on less firm ground than would be required for us to give orders to the Admiralty."

"But Miss Leverton says that the men on the scow were Blinder and Urquhart," Gregson said.

"Miss Leverton is not so credible a witness as one would wish. You will recall that in the eyes of the Americans, Miss Leverton remains a disgraced former Pinkerton employee with a grudge against Blinder." He paused. "What say you, Mycroft?"

Mycroft shook his head. "Regrettably, Blinder is an American with wealth and political influence. We would receive strong protests. I would not expect Her Majesty's government to risk that. Not when we are at war and there is an impending election."

"Do we have any other evidence to connect Blinder with the Whitehall incident?" asked the Commissioner.

Gregson and Jack shook their heads.

"Then we must await word from Lucy,"

* * *

Returning to Baker Street in our cab, I spoke to Holmes.

"You were quiet back there."

"I had nothing to say."

"You smiled when the medical report was read."

"Did I?"

"When Gregson said that all the tests had failed to identify a poison. You said the field had been narrowed."

"I suppose I did."

"Narrowed to what, then?"

He shrugged, but he said only, "That is what I propose to find out."

Chapter 25: Becky

"Mrs. Crabby works where?" Flynn was staring at her.

"Urquhart's pharmacy!" Becky's pulse was still skipping with excitement.

Her ploy to discover Moira's home address had worked perfectly. Well, not perfectly, in that she still didn't know where Moira and her mother actually lived. But she had approached the harried-looking woman in charge of the children's races, produced her own spare handkerchief, and explained earnestly that Moira had dropped it.

The woman had told her that Moira's last name was Dargie, and that her mother worked as a clerk behind the counter of Urquhart's, not far from here. Moira often helped out by making deliveries, and if Becky left the handkerchief at Urquhart's, someone would surely be able to return it to Moira even if she wasn't there today.

"That's a coincidence for you," Flynn said.

Becky studied his expression, which looked as though someone had just made him drink sour milk.

"What's the matter? This means that we were right—Moira's mother really could have something to hide, and whatever it is, it's connected to our case! Urquhart's shop isn't even far from here, it's over on—"

"Young Street," Flynn finished for her. "I know. Kevin took me over to look at the place this morning."

"And?" Becky said.

Flynn stuffed his hands into his pockets, shrugging. "And nothing. Just that I've learned that coincidences do happen sometimes when you're on a case. But they're not usually in your favour."

Becky frowned at him, but then copied his shrug. "Well, we still ought to go to visit Urquhart's. Kevin hasn't put in an appearance here at the fairgrounds, so Urquhart's really is our only lead."

"Right." Flynn still sounded about as happy as though he'd just pickpocketed a wooden shilling.

"We'll go back to the Inn so that I can change clothes," Becky said. "There's less chance of Moira's mother recognising me if I'm dressed differently. Then we'll go and see what we can find out."

* * *

It was amazing how differently Moira's mother treated you when she thought you were a paying customer.

Back at the Inn, Becky had changed into the frilliest dress she'd brought with her: white lace with a pink sash and a matching floppy pink bow for her hair. Becky wasn't especially fond of wearing either the dress or the bow, but they made for an effective cover. Mrs. Dargie hadn't recognised her, and moreover had swallowed Becky's story of shopping for a gift of perfume for her mother hook, line, and sinker.

The only real danger now was that Moira might put in an appearance, since she *would* recognise Becky, even dressed up like a layered wedding cake. But so far, Becky hadn't seen a sign of her, and Flynn was standing guard outside in the street.

He was dressed almost as nicely as she was—under

protest—but in the tweed jacket and cap and polished boots Mr. Holmes had given him, he could pass for a boy from a wealthy background. But he'd said that he'd rather stab himself with a rusty fork than pretend to shop for perfume, too.

Usually Becky wouldn't have accepted that as an excuse, but she had let him stay out of the act. This way, he could keep watch on the shop from out in the street and could warn her if Moira did arrive. Or if there was any sign of Urquhart.

"What about this one, dearie?" Mrs. Dargie asked, holding out another coloured glass bottle of scent.

There weren't any other customers in the shop at the moment, maybe because so many people were over watching the Highland Games.

Mrs. Dargie was smiling, but it was a fixed kind of smile, the kind that you pasted on and then forced yourself to hold in place.

Becky thought Mrs. Dargie still looked nervous, too. Her eyes darted around too much, and her muscles were all tense. Her hand shook a little as she unstoppered the perfume bottle.

"It's apple blossom."

Becky leaned forward and sniffed. "It's lovely. But I'm just not sure what my mother would like. What are those over there?"

She pointed to another row of bottles on a shelf along the wall with colourful printed labels.

"That's our own line of ladies' hair tonics. Very popular." Mrs. Dargie's eyes darted around the shop again, then refocused on Becky. "They're made right here in Inverness. We press the castor oil out of the beans ourselves and mix the tonics here at the shop from a special formula. Guaranteed to make your hair shine like a new penny."

"Castor oil?" Becky asked.

"Oh aye. Castor oil's verra' good for any number of ailments. A body can use it for rheumatics or bilious attacks or congestion in the lungs …"

"My mother doesn't have any of those."

"Well, no." Mrs. Dargie licked her lips. "But as I was saying, it's also verra' good for the hair. I'm sure your mother would be pleased if you were to give her a bottle to try."

She was speaking quickly, her words almost tripping over each other, but Becky had the impression that she wasn't actually paying very much attention to what she was saying. A swinging door stood in the wall right behind her, leading to what Becky assumed was the rear of the shop.

"Is that where you make all the tonics?" Becky tried to make her expression wide-eyed with interest as she pointed to the swinging door. "Can you show me? I would love to see how they're made!"

"Out of the question, I'm afraid, dear." Mrs. Dargie looked even more nervous as she shook her head. "Trade secrets, you know. Now, what about this perfume for your mother?" She picked up another bottle. "Lavender and primrose, this one is."

A sound came from somewhere in the back of the shop, as though an outside door had just opened and then closed again.

Mrs. Dargie jumped and turned a shade paler. Then she forced another tight smile.

"If you'll excuse me, dear, I've something to see to. I'll just be a moment, and you can think more about which perfume your mother might like."

She vanished through the door to the back room, which swung open and shut too fast for Becky to get more than a brief glimpse of whatever was back there. She thought she saw a long worktable and some kind of chemistry apparatus that looked a bit like Mr. Holmes's, but she couldn't be sure.

She was debating whether to risk going behind the counter and cracking the door open so that she could take another quick look when someone tapped her on the arm. She gasped and spun to find that Flynn had come into the shop to join her.

He looked tense, and what was more he didn't even make any kind of comment about her being jumpy.

"You need to get out of here." He spoke in a near soundless undertone. "Now."

"What? Why?" Becky asked. "Mrs. Dargie's going to think it's strange if I leave without buying a gift for my supposed mother after—"

"Yeah, what Mrs. Dargie thinks isn't on the list of things you should be worrying over right now," Flynn said, still in the same hushed whisper. "Urquhart's back there. At least I think he is. I saw him walk down the street and circle around the back of the shop."

Becky stared at him a moment, about to ask whether he was sure. But that was a stupid question. Of course Flynn was sure, otherwise he wouldn't have come in to tell her.

"Why do we need to leave, though?" she asked instead. "Urquhart doesn't know either of our faces. We might be able to find out something—"

Flynn cut her off, not by speaking but by grabbing hold of her arm and yanking her towards the door. Then he stopped short, so suddenly that Becky bumped into him.

A tall, weaselly-looking man was just coming into the shop. Urquhart. Becky had never seen him before, but from Flynn's description, it had to be him.

He was smiling a bit—a nasty, oily smile that sent sharp needles of cold into the pit of Becky's stomach. And he was holding a gun, levelled at her and Flynn.

Chapter 26: Lucy

"I'm sorry," Violet said.

"Sorry for what?"

The afternoon sun was high in the sky, warming the cobblestones under our feet. We were walking away from McGregor's pub and towards the distillery that the pub owner had told us was up the road. A few carriages rolled past, as well as a rustic-looking cart loaded down with passengers that had probably come into town from the outlying villages to watch the Highland Games.

Violet rubbed a hand up and down her cheek. "I'm sorry I was so little help back there—and that I completely destroyed our cover story about meeting friends. I promise you, I'm usually much better at prevarication."

"You've been through a great deal—" I started to say.

Violet cut me off, shaking her head. "No—I mean, yes, being kidnapped by Urquhart and Blinder was unpleasant. But if I'd wanted a pleasant life, I wouldn't have gone into the detective business. What's bothering me now is Preston."

"Preston?" I glanced at her in surprise. "Why? I thought he stayed behind in London with Holmes and Watson."

"He said that he was staying behind."

"You don't trust him?"

Violet laughed humourlessly. "That's something of

a complicated question. Do I trust him to do his utmost to track down a criminal and close a case? Absolutely. I would probably even trust him not to do anything he felt was morally wrong while solving said case. But would I trust him to be open about his plans? Not even remotely."

"You think he's carrying out his own line of investigation?"

"Preston is always carrying out his own line of investigation, even if he's working with you on the surface. But in this case, I think he's here in Inverness." She glanced at me. "I'm fairly sure that I saw him out on the street while we were inside McGregor's pub."

In the street, a boy on a bicycle darted out in front of a carriage, earning a shout from the policeman directing traffic.

"You think that Preston is following us?" I asked. I carefully kept all judgment out of my tone, but Violet still made a face.

"You think I'm being hysterical and imagining things. I don't blame you. In your place, I'd probably think exactly the same thing, especially since you scarcely know me." She sighed. "I'm not sure what I can say to convince you. I'm not even sure that I *should* convince you, since I can't be entirely certain that it really was Preston."

"What exactly did you see?"

"I was looking out of the door to McGregor's," Violet said. She frowned, clearly trying to cast her mind back to recall the details. "There were three men in bowler hats, two boys on bicycles, and a boy and girl playing at rolling hoops out in the street—"

"Wait a moment." I stopped her. "Why were you looking out of the door?"

Violet looked slightly surprised. "Why?"

"Yes. We were in the pub for the sole purpose of talking to

Mr. McGregor. There must have been something that made you turn back and look out into the road."

"You're right," Violet said slowly. "I'd been feeling on edge all morning. As though we were being watched—followed. I thought it was just the after effects of being kidnapped. You know, feeling nervy, because your imagination conjures up enemies lurking behind every corner."

I nodded. I did know, in fact.

Violet bit her lip, looking suddenly less certain. "But all morning I kept feeling convinced that if I looked behind me, I'd see Urquhart or Blinder."

"Did you?"

"Not a sign of them. But I did keep getting glimpses of a man in a green velvet coat and tartan kilt. One of the competitors at the Games, or so I assumed. Except that I saw him several times."

"You're certain it was the same man?"

"Fairly so. I never got a good look at his face. He always took care to be behind a crowd, or looking into a shop window. But he was missing a tassel on his … I don't know what they're called. Those leather and fur purse things that Scottish men wear around their waists when they're in a kilt."

"Sporran." I thought that was the correct term.

"Maybe." Violet waved a hand, dismissing the question. "At any rate, this man had one tassel too few on his, and I kept noticing it, every time that I saw him."

"You didn't say anything to me." I still kept any judgment out of my tone—or tried to—but Violet gave me a quick, apologetic glance all the same.

"I'm sorry. Honestly, I'm afraid I'm about as good at working with a partner as Preston—possibly even less. And I wasn't entirely sure whether the man was following us or whether it was just my nerves."

"You saw him again, though, outside of McGregor's pub?"

"I did. He walked past on the other side of the street as I was looking out of the door. I only got a quick glimpse of his face, but I did see it. And I'm fairly certain that it was Preston."

"Preston, dressed up in traditional Scottish highland garb?"

I was trying to visualise the Pinkerton agent abandoning his corduroy jacket and string tie for a kilt and knee-high stockings—and failing spectacularly.

"I know." Violet bit her lip. "It sounds ridiculous. But Preston is quite good at disguising himself to look like someone else. He doesn't advertise the fact, but that lazy cowboy act of his is just that—an act. It's part of what makes him so skilled as an agent. No one expects him to be anything different from who he appears to be, so they're caught off guard when he proves them wrong."

That sounded more than a little like Holmes.

I studied Violet, considering everything that she'd just told me. There was always a chance that she really was just letting frayed nerves run away with her. But I didn't think so. She was right; I hardly knew her at all, but everything I did know had shown her to be a capable agent, and she clearly had an eye for observing details.

"If Preston really is in Inverness, why wouldn't he let us know? Why resort to covertly shadowing us?"

"I don't know." Violet shook her head in frustration. "Except that he always prefers to play a lone hand, as I say."

"Could that lead him into trouble?"

"It could lead anyone into trouble, as I've rather graphically demonstrated over the course of the past few days." A wry half-smile quirked up the corner of Violet's mouth. "I've known Preston to take risks, although never unnecessary ones. He's fairly level-headed and extremely controlled on the whole. But on the other hand, the cases he works aren't usually personal."

"You mean the connection to his sister's poisoning?" If Preston blamed Blinder for ruining his sister's life, that could certainly make him less than impartial.

"Yes." Violet seemed on the verge of saying something more, but then appeared to think again, closing her mouth instead.

I debated for another second or two, but then made up my mind. "All right. In that case, I think that I had better go and speak to Mrs. Campbell at her distillery alone, while you come up with a plan for locating Preston."

CHAPTER 27: BECKY

Becky's heart pounded. Fear choked her, making it hard to breathe.

Mr. Urquhart stepped forward into the shop, keeping the gun trained on them. He shut the door, locking it with one hand and then flipping the sign in the window from open to closed.

"Now. Here's what we're going to do." He spoke softly, but with a menacing edge to his tone. "The two of ye are going to sit down in those chairs over there"—he gestured to a pair of wooden chairs set out for waiting customers near the counter where medicines and herbal cures were prepared.

Becky darted a glance towards the swinging door to the back room, but there was no sign of Mrs. Dargie. She probably wouldn't care what happened to them anyway, or else she'd be too terrified to be any help.

Mr. Urquhart kept speaking. "Then we're going to have a nice little chat about what yer doing here and how much ye know. So move."

He gestured with the gun, herding them towards the wooden chairs.

Flynn looked sideways at Becky. "We'd better do as he says. No use being a baby about it."

Becky was tempted to snap that she didn't need his hints, she'd have thought of that plan for herself. But that would alert Urquhart, so she just nodded instead.

Then she took a step towards Urquhart, clasping her hands in front of her. "Oh, p-please."

Becky was very good at being able to cry on command by now. She had practiced and practiced before a mirror, because Lucy always said that the more people underestimated you, the more surprised they were when you beat them.

"Please, don't hurt us!" she wailed. "We'll tell you anything you like!"

Urquhart's face pinched in distaste. "Stop snivelling, girl!" he barked.

Becky wailed louder.

"Stop it, I say!"

For a brief second, Urquhart was focused on her instead of on Flynn, and Flynn hadn't been an expert pickpocket for nothing. Out of the corner of her eye, Becky saw his hand shoot out, lightning-quick, and snatch something off of one of the shelves in the beauty section—something small enough that he was able to palm it and hide it under the cuff of his sleeve.

Urquhart still had a gun, and all they had were whatever random cosmetics Flynn had been able to sneak, but Becky felt slightly better all the same. They'd faced worse odds and still come out all right.

Urquhart looked at Flynn. "Get over there, or I'll shoot your weepy little friend."

Wordlessly, Flynn obeyed, walking over to the set of wooden chairs.

Urquhart fumbled one-handed in his pocket, extracting a length of cord, then grabbed hold of Becky's arm. He dragged her over to the chairs, too, and set her down hard in the one next to Flynn's, all the while keeping his gun aimed right at her chest.

She'd hoped they might have an opening if he planned to tie them up, but instead he thrust the rope at Flynn.

"Tie her wrists," Urquhart commanded. "And no funny business about the knots, mind. I'm watching ye."

"Right," Flynn said. His eyes met Becky's.

This time, she didn't want to risk nodding. She was already taking a risk that Urquhart would notice how abruptly she'd stopped crying, but she couldn't spare enough attention to muster up more tears.

She held Flynn's gaze to show that she understood and tensed, ready.

Flynn moved behind her, holding the rope, and looped it around her wrists. Urquhart was watching every move he made, but Becky saw him relax just a tiny fraction after Flynn had secured the first knot.

Now or never.

Flynn knew it, too. He gave a cough, which they hadn't worked out beforehand, but Becky knew it was a signal all the same.

She threw herself to the right, just as he'd told her to, opening the way for Flynn to haul off and throw whatever he'd pinched off the shelves straight into Urquhart's face.

He'd chosen a jar of face powder—which couldn't have been a better pick. The powder exploded in Urquhart's face in a choking, blinding cloud.

Urquhart reeled back, coughing and clawing at his eyes. Flynn knocked the gun out of his hand, sending it clattering across the floor.

Becky jumped up. Her wrists were tied, but she grabbed hold of the chair with her joined hands and swung it in a whistling arc at Urquhart's head.

The sturdy wooden seat connected with the back of Urquhart's skull. He staggered, then collapsed to the ground, moaned once, then lay still.

Flynn yanked the rope off of Becky's wrists and bent down to fasten it around Urquhart's, tying his hands behind his back. Then he found another length of cord in Urquhart's coat pocket and used it to secure Urquhart's ankles.

"He may be good at chemistry, but he's not very bright," Becky said, watching. "He doesn't even know that you should always tie your prisoner *to* the chair, not just in the chair."

"Never mind that." Flynn finished yanking the ropes tight and stood up. "What now?"

Becky hesitated. The fear that still knotted her stomach was telling her to run. But that wouldn't get them any closer to having answers for Lucy and Mr. Holmes.

"Moira's mother went into the back of the shop," she said.

"Well, she's either gone now or else she's deaf," Flynn said.

That was true. After all the noise they'd made knocking out Mr. Urquhart, surely she would have at the very least opened the door to see what was happening.

Becky looked down at Urquhart. His head was lolling back, his mouth half open. He'd be unconscious for at least long enough for them to search the back room, if they could.

"Let's have a look," she said. "We can always run if we have to."

Flynn pushed open the swinging door, tense, poised on the balls of his feet in case they did have to turn around and make a fast getaway. But once he'd got the door fully open, he relaxed.

"No one's here."

Becky came up beside him to have a look. He was right. The back room wasn't large, just a single square space, with shelves lining all four walls. The shelves were filled with an array of glass bottles and jars like the ones out in the shop, except that these didn't have labels pasted onto them yet.

A door in the back wall opened into what through the window looked to be a narrow alleyway. Becky assumed that must be how Mrs. Dargie had left.

A worktable stood against the wall to their right, holding a big metal contraption: a large pipe about the width of a cricket bat, with valves and levers on top.

"That must be where they press the castor beans," Becky murmured. The shop might be empty, but somehow, she still felt as though she should be whispering.

Flynn let the door swing shut behind them. "Castor beans?"

"Castor oil's good for lots of different complaints, or so Mrs. Dargie told me," Becky said. "They press the beans here—squeeze the oil out, I suppose that means—and then turn it into poultices and hair tonics and that sort of thing." She wrinkled her nose. "It smells like a gin palace in here."

She'd sniffed so many different perfumes while talking with Mrs. Dargie that it had taken her a moment or two to notice, but the air in here was sharp with the smell of some kind of alcohol.

"You're right." Flynn frowned, but before he could say anything more, a sound came from behind them in the front room of the shop: first the scrape of a key in a lock, then the squeak of hinges as the front door opened.

Becky looked at Flynn, wide-eyed, he looked back at her, and then they both nodded at the same time.

Without having to say a word, they sprinted for the back door, yanked it open, and a moment later were pelting down the narrow cobblestone alley outside.

They ran all the way down the alley, turned, and ran down another, made several turns, then walked for several blocks on a busier street full of crowds of morning shoppers, doubled back, looked into shop windows, and used all of Mr. Holmes's other tricks to be sure that no one was following.

Then, finally, Flynn slowed down and said, "I think we're in the clear."

They were on a quieter side street, walking past neat rows of terraced brick houses with nicely swept front steps and flower pots in the windows.

Becky slowed her steps to match his, catching her breath. "I suppose this is what you meant about coincidences not usually working out in your favour?"

"Something like that," Flynn agreed. "Seemed like a bit much that the girl who happened to talk to you at the games has a mother who works at Urquhart's."

"You think Moira singled me out on purpose?" Becky thought about that. She'd have sworn that Moira was genuine, but she supposed you never knew. Now that she thought about it, the other girl had known that Becky was a visitor at the inn.

"Someone knew that we were going to be visiting Urquhart's pharmacy," Flynn said. "Could have been her. Could have been Kevin. He could have gone straight to Urquhart and probably got more than a shilling for telling him all about me."

"Or it could have been Mrs. Dargie," Becky said. "She could have only pretended not to recognise me. I heard someone come in through the rear entrance of the shop while I was there, and right after that Mrs. Dargie made an excuse to go back. It could have been Urquhart. He could have told her to make herself scarce while he dealt with us. And it was all pointless!" The words had a nasty taste in Becky's mouth. "Urquhart's bound to have got away by now. Whoever we heard coming into the shop would have untied him."

"I wonder if it was Blinder," Flynn said.

"Maybe. Either way, Urquhart's gone, we can't risk going back to the shop, not now. And we didn't even find out anything useful, except that castor oil is good for rheumatism and making your hair shiny!"

"That's not all castor oil's good for."

There was a note in Flynn's voice that made Becky give him a quick look.

"What do you mean?"

"Don't you remember the lecture Mr. Holmes gave us a couple of months back on poisons?"

Becky frowned. "Which part?"

She and Flynn had tutors for subjects like history and grammar, but Mr. Holmes always taught their chemistry and science lessons himself.

"What he told us about ricin."

"Ricin? Oh!" Becky looked at Flynn, wide-eyed, as parts of the lecture started to come back to her. "You're right, it's made from—"

"Castor beans," Flynn finished for her. "Exactly. You use alcohol to precipitate the toxins out, and that's how ricin's made."

Becky knew that there'd been more to Mr. Holmes's lecture than that, but right now she cared less about recalling the details than she did about where all of this was leading.

"So Urquhart and Blinder could be using the pharmacy as a cover to produce ricin?" She thought of the apparatus they'd seen in the back room, all the glass bottles and jars. A shiver twisted through her. "That's a lot of poison."

"Exactly."

"But why would they want to produce that much ricin? And what does any of this have to do with a monster on the Loch and a bomb destroying a London water main?"

She was trying to remember what else Mr. Holmes had told them about how ricin acted as a poison. It was a fairly slow killer, she remembered that, not like cyanide or strychnine. Inhaling ricin would eventually cause your lungs to fill up with fluid. Ingesting it would cause your internal organs to fail.

"I don't know what they'd want that much poison for," Flynn said. "Except that I'd go out on a limb and guess it can't be anything good. As for the monster, though—" He glanced at her.

Becky nodded agreement before he could even finish the thought. "We ought to send a telegram to Mr. Holmes and tell him what we've learned first, though."

"About Urquhart's?"

"About Urquhart's and the castor oil and everything. What's wrong?" Becky asked. There was a deep furrow between Flynn's brows.

"I was just thinking. If you were Urquhart, and you'd just been knocked out in your own shop, what's the first thing you'd do?"

"Try to catch us." Which Urquhart and Blinder hadn't—not yet, anyway.

"Sure, but after that."

Becky finally saw where Flynn was leading. "I'd probably check with the Inn, to find out where we're staying. And then I'd go to the telegraph offices to see whether we'd sent any messages back to London." She looked at Flynn, uneasiness squirming through her. "You think Urquhart will be there, if we try to send a telegram?"

"It's a possibility."

The busy street all around them suddenly seemed much less safe than it had a moment before. "We can write up the message and ask someone else to send it."

"We can, and that's probably our smartest move," Flynn agreed. "But we've got to allow for the possibility that Urquhart or Blinder might get their hands on the message that we send."

"Telegrams are private, though."

Flynn snorted. "You think that's going to stop a bloke like Blinder from throwing his money about and getting the telegraph clerk to show him what we've sent?"

"No." Becky could imagine it all too clearly. "All right. So we make sure that our message doesn't say anything important. Or at least that it doesn't *seem* to say anything important. But we find a way to tell Mr. Holmes what he needs to know all the same. Do you have a paper and pencil?"

Flynn dug in his pocket and eventually produced a stub of a pencil and a slightly crumpled and grubby sheet of paper torn from a notebook.

They worked for several minutes over the wording, then nodded agreement that the message was as well written as they could make it.

"Now. Let's find a likely person to hand this in for us," Becky said. "And then let's take a trip out to the Loch and see if we can do any monster spotting for ourselves."

CHAPTER 28: VIOLET

Violet walked up and down cobblestone streets at random, scarcely seeing the quaint architecture or the plaid blankets and tins of shortbread and woollen sweaters displayed in shop windows.

Lucy had told her to come up with a plan for locating Preston, but that was proving to be easier said than done. She hadn't yet seen a single sign of him, and the best plan she could come up with was to wait and see whether he started following her again.

She even wandered into some of the shops, making a useless purchase or two, as well as a few more useful ones.

No one approached her. No one besides the shop clerks spoke to her.

After more than two hours of walking around Inverness and achieving nothing but increasingly sore feet, she was beginning to wonder whether Preston was in fact here, as opposed to being once more just a figment of Violet's own overwrought imagination.

Lucy had been amazingly ready to believe Violet's story of having seen Preston, for which Violet was grateful. But Violet hadn't been entirely open about the raggedness of her own nerves.

She'd mentioned to Lucy that she was still feeling on edge. But she hadn't described the sick, hollow feeling that persisted in the pit of her stomach, or the tension that still knotted her muscles every time a carriage rattled past them in the street.

And she hadn't told Lucy, either, about the interludes on the boat with Blinder and Urquhart, when she'd imagined Preston being there. But she couldn't have hallucinated his presence in kilt, sporran, and stockings outside of McGregor's.

Or could she?

Violet was getting thoroughly sick of mistrusting her own mind.

Throughout her life, whatever had been ripped away—whether it was her parents or her childhood home or her job at Pinkerton's—she'd always been able to depend on herself and her own intelligence. Now, wondering whether she could trust her perceptions was a new and entirely unpleasant experience.

Maybe Preston had decided to follow Lucy instead of her. Maybe—

Stop.

Violet forcibly snapped off her train of thought before she could circle back yet again to whether the man who'd followed them all morning had in fact been Preston.

She took brief stock of her surroundings, then marched up the steps of the large, gothic style brick church that she realised was directly in front of her.

Why not? She and Lucy had intended to inquire at both the pubs and the churches about their trio of missing persons. As long as she was stuck trekking around Inverness in the vain hope that Preston would eventually decide to shadow her again, she might as well try to learn something of use to the investigation.

A sign near the door read, *Cathedral Church of Saint Andrew*. Violet pushed open the big wooden front door and stepped into the nave.

It was a beautiful church. The floor was inlaid with a pattern of gold and brown. Stone columns held up a vaulted ceiling.

Stained glass windows along the aisles let in coloured shafts of light.

Her grandfather would have loved it. He'd been a professor of medieval literature at Harvard, and everything about the place would have appealed to his sensibilities. Actually, he'd have loved Inverness as a whole. He'd been to Europe as a young man, but had never been able to afford to go back—

"Good afternoon."

The deep man's voice made Violet spin around to find that a man in the flowing white cassock of an Episcopal priest had stepped out of the shadows of one of the pillars.

He looked to be somewhere about sixty, bald, with a fringe of white hair around his ears and a bushy white beard. His face was strong-boned, but had a good-humoured, kindly look as he regarded Violet, hands lightly clasped in front of him.

"May I help you?"

"I—thank you." Violet silently cursed both Preston and her own impulsiveness. In her determination to stop thinking about Preston, she had come in here without giving a thought to what she was going to say. "I'm a visitor here. For the Highland Games," she added.

"Ah." The priest looked at her with interest. "American?"

"Yes."

"You're a long way from home."

That was probably true in more senses besides just the geographical, but Violet had had her fill of introspection for one day.

"Is this your church?" she asked. "It's quite beautiful."

"I am the Reverend Webb, provost here. And thank you, I find it so." He looked around the place with affection. "I served a church in South Africa for many years, and much as I loved it there, I find that I am equally enamoured of the Scottish Highlands."

That explained his accent, which was neither Scottish nor English, but had a colonial twang.

Violet pulled herself together and manufactured a smile. She had interviewed thieves and murderers and gone undercover to infiltrate a group of violent anarchists over the course of her career as a detective. She could manage a conversation with an elderly clergyman.

"Actually, I'm writing a piece for our local newspaper back home about my trip to Scotland," she said. "All about the history and traditions of the Highlands, that sort of thing. I understand that there's a legend about a monster in the Loch here?"

"Oh, indeed yes." The Reverend Webb smiled comfortably. "There is mention of it—or at least of a water creature—in an ancient chronicle about the Life of St. Columba."

"By Adomnán?" Violet asked.

Reverend Webb looked surprised. "You are familiar with his writings?"

"Only a bit. My grandfather was, though."

Her grandfather really would have loved it here.

"In that case, you will know that Adomnán's *Life of Saint Columba* was written in the sixth century AD, but the events he chronicled took place about a century earlier. According to Adomnán, Saint Columba was staying in the land of the Picts with his companions when he encountered a group of locals carrying out funeral rites for a man by the River Ness. Upon inquiry, the local residents explained that the man had been mauled and dragged underwater by a 'water beast' while swimming in the river. Columba called on one of his followers, an

Irishman called Luigne moccu Min, to swim across the river. The water beast drew near to Luigne, but Saint Columba made the sign of the cross and said: 'Go no further. Do not touch the man. Go back at once.' Whereupon the monster fled—*as though it had been pulled back with ropes* is how Adomnán puts it. The story ends with Columba's men and the Picts giving thanks for a miracle. Of course, such stories are quite common in the old church chronicles. The priest calling in divine forces to subdue the reptilian dragon."

"Fascinating," Violet said.

Behind them, the church door opened again, and an elderly man with a bent back and a thatch of shaggy white hair hobbled in, leaning heavily on a cane. He shuffled slowly up one of the side aisles and finally settled in a pew near the altar, where he bowed his head in prayer.

"And have there been any more recent sightings of the monster?" Violet asked Reverend Webb.

"Oh yes. It seems that once every ten or twenty years, someone reports seeing a strange creature in the water. In the late 1880s, I believe a local man claimed to have seen a monster that looked something like a giant salamander." He smiled gently. "Whether any of them has actually seen anything more than a floating log enhanced by a drop of too much whisky, I cannot say."

"And now?" Violet asked. "I thought I'd heard in town that some people were claiming to have seen the monster in the past few months."

For the first time, a shadow crossed Reverend Webb's expression. "I have heard the rumours, as well. Although I cannot believe that there is any real substance to them. As a man of science, as well as faith, I cannot honestly entertain the possibility that a giant sea monster haunts the Loch. But I do fear the kind of mass hysteria that such stories can cause. The tales I have heard are that the monster carries some kind of dread disease, and is somehow poisoning the local water supply."

"Really?" The back of Violet's neck prickled. "Do you know how the rumours got started?"

"I imagine in the same way that most such rumours do. Someone sees a floating log or an unusually large eel and mistakes it for a water creature. They speak of it to a friend or relation, who carries the tale further, adding and embellishing for dramatic effect. Add that to a few people dying of the kind of fevers and other illnesses that are sadly all too common during the summer, and before long, the entire city of Inverness and the surrounding counties are afire with stories of a plague-ridden monster."

Violet doubted that the matter was anywhere near that simple—or that innocent, either. But she smiled and nodded.

"I imagine that you're right. Well, thank you so much for speaking with me and for the lesson on local history. My readers back home will be so interested to hear all about Loch Ness."

Violet walked up the cathedral's central aisle after taking her leave of Reverend Webb, pushing through the big double front doors and back out into the open air.

The sun was sinking lower on the horizon, the heat of the day burning down to the cool of early evening. Instead of continuing down the church's front steps, Violet sidestepped, plastering herself to the brick wall beside the door.

She didn't have long to wait. No more than a minute later, the cathedral doors opened again, and the elderly man who'd shuffled in during her conversation with Reverend Webb came hobbling out, still leaning heavily on his cane.

Violet hesitated, but only for a moment.

Evening was falling, shrouding the church entrance in deep shadow, and there was for the moment no one passing by in the road to act as witness.

As the old man started down the front steps, she moved out of her place of concealment, wrapped her forearm across his throat, and yanked him backwards.

One of her useful purchases in the Inverness shops had been a dagger of sorts, a *sgian dubh*, the clerk had called it. The hilt was made of bone, inlaid with decorative designs of Celtic knotwork, but the blade was perfectly functional and wickedly sharp.

Violet set the edge against the elderly man's throat.

"I wouldn't make any sudden moves if I were you."

The man froze, then, after taking a long moment, he slowly raised his hands in a gesture of surrender.

He turned his head—which made the shaggy white wig slip to one side—and Preston's familiar blue gaze met hers.

"Not planning to."

Chapter 29: Lucy

Mrs. Campbell was a tall, thin woman in her middle fifties, with grey hair and an anxious, care-worn face.

I had found the front entrance to Campbell's Distillery locked, and only after several minutes of knocking had Mrs. Campbell finally answered. Now she stood in the front entrance of the distillery with her head a little thrown back, as though she were trying to prevent me from seeing anything inside, and she certainly hadn't invited me to come in.

"We're closed." She spoke abruptly, and looked ready to step back inside and slam the door in my face.

"Oh, what a shame." I smiled pleasantly. "I represent a restaurant in London. Our customers want an authentic taste of the Highlands, and we seek a working relationship with a Scottish distillery. I was hoping that you might be interested in supplying us with whisky."

I could see caution and a flicker of hope warring in Mrs. Campbell's expression. But she shook her head.

"I'm afraid we'd not be able to help. As I said, we're closed. Haven't made any whisky in months, now."

"But you have all the equipment, surely."

There was complicated machinery visible behind her: huge copper boilers and rows of big wooden vats.

"Well, aye, we do." She cast a quick, nervous glance over her shoulder, then smoothed her apron down with work-reddened hands. "But we're only making grain alcohol these days. For local businesses."

"Oh yes. I think I'd heard that you supply Urquhart's pharmacy, don't you?"

I hadn't of course heard any such thing, but I wanted to see how Mrs. Campbell reacted to the name.

"Well—" Her face blanched and her eyes darted about as though she were scrambling to find a way to prevaricate. But whatever else Mrs. Campbell might be, she definitely wasn't terribly practiced at coming up with a convincing lie. "Well, yes, yes we do supply them, that's true," she said. "They use the alcohol in their patent medicines—as a solvent for the herbs and such."

"And your children?" I asked. "I'd heard that they work with you in the business, is that right?"

"Well—" Mrs. Campbell licked her lips. "Aye, they did at one time. But I … haven't seen them just lately."

"Do you know where they might be?"

Mrs. Campbell's eyes darted around again and then she shook her head. "I dinna' think … that is … no, I haven't seen them lately. I think they're working out of town."

I took a breath, guilt pinching in the pit of my stomach. Trying to break down anyone as pathetically bad at resisting even the mildest interrogation techniques as Mrs. Campbell was felt worse than shooting fish in a barrel. And if I was right, she was about to have the worst day of her life. I hadn't taken her children away, but I was about to be the one to break the news to her.

"Mrs. Campbell, I'm afraid that I wasn't telling you the truth before." If I was about to shatter her world apart, the very least

I could do was be as honest as possible about it. "I'm actually a private detective, looking into the deaths of three people who were found in London."

"Deaths?" Mrs. Campbell's lips shaped the word, but no sound emerged.

"Yes." I spoke gently, although there was no real way of softening this blow. "Two young men and a woman. We have reason to believe that they were your sons and daughter."

Mrs. Campbell stared at me a moment, and then her face crumpled.

"I knew it." She pressed a fold of her apron against her mouth, trying to contain her sobs, but they still fought free. Her shoulders shook. "I knew something was wrong when I didna' hear from them. Not a word, for weeks and weeks. I've been so afraid … but I never thought … they're dead?"

She looked at me imploringly, as though begging me to say that it was all a misunderstanding. I'd seen that same expression on the faces of so many bereaved family members: the desperate wish to believe that at any moment they might wake up from the nightmare into which they'd just been plunged.

"I'm so sorry," I said. "If you feel up to it, I have some photographs I can show you. But if you'd rather not—"

"No." Tears were still rolling down Mrs. Campbell's cheeks, but she shook her head and said, with an edge of desperation, "No. I've been afraid—so afraid—all these weeks. I need to know. Dead or alive, I canna' live one more day without knowing what's become of them."

I could understand that. "Maybe you'd like to sit down?"

Mrs. Campbell shook her head again, mopping her eyes with the corner edge of her apron. "No. Just show me."

I took out the mortuary photographs that Holmes had obtained for me before our trip here.

Mrs. Campbell barely glanced at them before her tears burst forth again. "Aye, it's them." She was still weeping, but the words came out in a flood in between sobs, as though they'd been pent up for too long and now had to break free. "They told me that they'd been hired on for a new job—one that would pay well, but meant they had to work at a secret factory. They couldna' even tell me where they'd be."

I hated to ask her anything just now, but I had to put the question, "Did you—or they—think that was odd?"

"Aye." Mrs. Campbell tried to staunch the flow of her tears. "Aye, I think we all knew deep down that something wasna' right about it all. But we needed the money so badly, if we were to begin making the whisky again." Her voice wavered.

"Do you have any idea who it was who hired them?"

"No. They never said, and I never asked." Mrs. Campbell looked down at the photographs in her hands, her eyes swimming with another flood of tears. "So off they went, my boys and my girl. They went at night, and they had to take a boat to get to where they were going, I know that much. I worried, though I knew it was foolishness, because there'd been rumours goin' about of the Loch monster."

Chapter 30: Violet

Preston swallowed, then winced. Violet still hadn't removed the knife blade from his throat, though she was keeping the pressure light enough not to break the skin.

"I can explain," he said.

"Oh, you're going to. Beginning with why you're here in Inverness and ending with what you think you're doing following me."

Instead of answering, though, Preston glanced down at Violet's knife hand and raised an eyebrow. The gathering twilight leached the colour from his face, turning his craggy features into a pattern of light and shadow.

"How did you know it was me?"

"I didn't."

One side of Preston's mouth quirked up. "I see. Do I want to know what you were planning to do if you wound up assaulting a perfectly innocent elderly church-goer?"

"Chalk that up as an average day?"

Violet slid the knife back into the sheath and pocketed both. Without the element of surprise, she wasn't terribly confident in her ability to keep hold of the weapon if Preston decided to try to get it away from her.

"And now for that explanation?"

She could see the brief debate taking place behind Preston's gaze, but then he said, "I'm here because I'm following up a lead on Urquhart."

"Oh, thank you so much for that astonishing revelation," Violet said. She was suddenly regretting having put away the knife. "Also, we're currently in the month of July and the earth is round?"

Preston gave her a full-fledged grin this time. "Feel like sharing any of your own information?"

Violet tried to ignore the way Preston's smile—for once genuine and unguarded—made her insides dip and swoop.

"Would the lead you're following have anything to do with Campbell's distillery?" she asked.

She saw surprise register in Preston's gaze. "So you've found out about the link to Campbell's?"

"Via a chatty pub owner, yes. Is that how you discovered that our three dead bodies are probably brothers and a sister from that family?"

"Are they now?" Preston spoke slowly, as though fitting new pieces of a puzzle together inside his head. Which meant that not only had Violet not received any information, she had just given some away for free.

"How did you find out about Campbell's?"

She was fully expecting that Preston would refuse to answer, but instead he said, "I found the carriage that carried you to the docks abandoned in a back alley in Limehouse. There was the scrap of what looked like a receipt on the floor from a payment made to a distillery on Academy Street, Inverness, Scotland. I asked around and the only distillery with that address is Campbell's."

Violet couldn't imagine how much patience and dogged determination it must have taken to find one abandoned carriage in a city the size of London.

"So why are you here, then?" she asked. "And not on Academy Street? Or have you already been?"

Preston's gaze shifted. The expression that crossed his face was so completely foreign to everything Violet knew about him that it took her a moment to even identify what it was. But it was embarrassment. Preston was embarrassed by her question.

Finally, he said, "I was outside the Inn this morning. There was a man there who looked to be watching the place."

Two distinct reactions went through Violet in the same instant: a jolt of reflexive fear as she recalled the way Urquhart had fondled the blade of the ax, and incredulity.

Incredulity won.

"You were worried about me?"

Worried enough to have spent the entire day tailing her in various disguises.

Preston looked down, then back up at her, a brief gleam of rueful humour in his gaze.

"Awkward, am I right?"

It was more than awkward, it was … Violet couldn't even put a name to what it was, nor did she want to stop and consider it for too long just now. She was used to every encounter with Preston giving her ample reasons to dislike him.

She was already feeling off-balance enough as it was. If her justifiable indignation at Preston collapsed under her, she wasn't sure she would be able to remain standing.

"The man you saw outside the Inn," she asked. "Was it Urquhart?"

Preston shook his head. "No. It was a fellow I didn't recognise. Average height, blond hair, somewhere in his thirties."

He'd just described half the population of Scotland. Still, Violet had to stop herself from reflexively looking around to see whether there was anyone who looked like that hanging about now, peering at them from under one of the decorative shrubs that surrounded the church or loitering in the street.

"Have you seen the man since this morning?" she asked.

Preston shook his head. "No sign of him."

"It sounds as though your day was about as productive as mine," Violet said.

Preston's one-sided grin flashed out again, but then he seemed to hesitate before saying, "I did get another lead on Urquhart. One that I think is worth following up."

"Oh? What is it?"

"I don't want to say just yet."

"Really. Why am I not surprised?" At least she was no longer in danger of losing hold of her annoyance with Preston.

"Because it could be dangerous," Preston continued as though she hadn't spoken. "I want to check into a few things on my own first before bringing anyone else in."

Really, that was equally insulting: the implication that she would be unable to cope if a situation turned dangerous. But all the same, instead of arguing, Violet found herself saying, "Be careful out there. Blinder and Urquhart are nasty customers. Try not to get yourself killed."

The words startled Preston almost as much as they did her. She saw surprise flicker at the back of his gaze, then he said, "I'll tell you what. Meet me later tonight at that pub—McGregor's—and I'll explain everything."

Ordinarily, Violet would have asked whether she had the word *idiot* printed on her forehead if he thought she was going to believe that.

But instead she said, again, "Just be careful. Going off alone isn't often the safest choice."

"Maybe." Preston pushed off from the church wall. The indolent cowboy act lifted for a brief moment, and Violet caught a glimpse of the man underneath: lean, hardened, and with the inherent, graceful menace of a predator. "But I've never lost yet."

"I know." The evening air wasn't particularly chilly, but cold prickled across Violet's skin all the same. "Just remember that there's a first time for everything."

Chapter 31: Watson

A light knock sounded at the door of our sitting room on Baker Street.

Holmes was at his laboratory table, measuring chemicals. He called out, "Not now, Mrs. Hudson!"

The door opened, nonetheless, and I saw our grey-haired landlady at the entrance. Her diminutive frame partially blocked my view, but I could see someone was behind her.

"I know you're busy, Mr. Holmes," she said, "but this gentleman was most insistent. And I believe it has to do with something you're working on. I have his business card."

She held it in her outstretched hand.

"Watson," said Holmes, his eyes fixed upon a beaker he was filling with a clear blue liquid.

I stepped forward to take the card. As I did so, I took notice of our visitor, standing behind Mrs. Hudson and barely as tall. A businesslike man of perhaps forty-five years, he held a bowler hat before him in both hands. A fringe of neatly trimmed greying hair circled the crown of his small, bald head. Behind a pair of gold wire-rimmed spectacles, his clear blue eyes widened with what I perceived as hope and expectation.

I read aloud from the card. "Eric Polder. Manager, Hampton Water Treatment Works."

"Ah," said Holmes. "Thank you, Mrs. Hudson. Dr. Watson,

please show Mr. Polder to a chair. I shall be with you in a moment."

While Holmes finished making notations in his book and putting away his chemicals, I seated our visitor on the chair I normally occupied on my side of the hearth. Soon Holmes was with us, taking his usual chair on the other side.

"Now Mr. Polder. What have you to tell me?"

"I need you to come out to the works, as quickly as you can. I am at my wits' end, sir!"

"Come to Hampton? To do what?"

"Why to investigate our operations. I need to be certain I have not missed something. The reporters have been hounding me. They scoff at my assurances! But I tell you I have honestly done everything I can—"

"To prevent cholera?" Holmes asked.

Polder's hand went to his mouth. "Why, of course, did I not say? Please forgive me the oversight, I have been so distracted—"

"Why are the reporters hounding you? Has there been an outbreak of cholera?"

"I confess I do not know the particulars. But reporters from five different newspapers have called on my office. They claim contaminated water is being supplied to innocent citizens in the South London area."

"And your plant supplies that area?"

"Through the Southwark and Vauxhall Company. We supply water to them and to three other companies who service three other locales. You see, we have a reservoir for each one, each covering several acres, and our sand filtration—"

Holmes held up his hand.

"Which reporters, please? Have you their cards?"

Mr. Polder seemed taken aback. "Why, no. I did not take them. My assistant did. But I should like you to examine the reservoirs, and our laboratory, where we do our purification tests. We are very proud of our work, and you as a man of chemistry and science—"

He stopped, because Holmes had risen from his chair and crossed over to our telephone table. He picked up the receiver and spoke into the mouthpiece. "Get me the Hampton Water Treatment Works, Mr. Polder's office," he told the operator. A few moments elapsed. Then Holmes spoke, his voice crisp and authoritative. "Are you Mr. Polder's assistant? This is Sherlock Holmes. Mr. Polder is with me. Do you have the cards of the reporters who visited him yesterday? Of course. Here he is."

He passed the instrument over to our visitor. "She wants to verify that you wish her to cooperate."

"Of course I wish it!" Polder said into the mouthpiece. He seemed flustered, perhaps due to the strain he had been under, or perhaps not accustomed to Holmes's direct manner.

Whatever the reason, however, he made himself clear to his assistant and she in turn provided a name, which Holmes asked me to record:

L. G. Rittenhouse, of the *Penny Illustrated*.

"Just the one name? Only one card? Very well. Thank you, Miss Brinkley."

He hung up the receiver.

"Seems odd that the others wouldn't leave a card," said Mr. Polder.

"On the contrary," said Holmes.

"Very well, if you say so," said our guest. "Now, can you please come with me to the Works in Hampton? Dr. Watson, you would be welcome as well. I am so very anxious to get this cleared up—"

Holmes stood, replaced the telephone instrument on our table, and remained standing. His words were modulated with the patient tones one might take with a child. "Mr. Polder. Who suggested you call upon me?"

"Why, Mr. Maxwell. He's one of the directors. On the company board."

"You told him of the inquiries from reporters?"

"Why, yes, sir. It's part of my job to see to it that the company reputation—"

"Yes, yes. Why did Mr. Maxwell say to consult me?"

Polder sat silent for a long moment, clasping and unclasping his hands. "He said it would be good for business, Mr. Holmes," he said. "Bringing you in to give us the seal of approval, so to speak."

"Something to tell reporters?"

"Yes, sir."

"So they would refrain from criticising you, and instead direct their attentions to me?"

Polder bit his lower lip and looked down at his boots.

Holmes stepped over to our sitting-room door and opened it. "You can tell your Mr. Maxwell that I decline to become embroiled in your company's affairs. Good day to you, Mr. Polder."

I stood up and escorted Mr. Polder to the door. When he had gone, I shut the door and turned to Holmes.

I was surprised to find him smiling, our telephone receiver once again in his hand.

"It begins, Watson!" he said. Then into the telephone, he said, "Inspector Gregson, please. This is Sherlock Holmes."

A moment later, he was speaking to Gregson. "Two avenues of investigation, Inspector. First, question one L. G. Rittenhouse, a reporter for the Penny Illustrated, and find out what caused him to visit the Hampton Water Treatment Works yesterday. Second, determine if any cases of cholera have been reported in London this week."

Chapter 32: Lucy

"I don't think Preston is coming," Violet said.

We were seated near the huge stone fireplace of McGregor's pub. Violet had been drumming her fingers on our tabletop and glancing at the clock on the wall practically from the moment that we had sat down. But by now, I was inclined to agree with her.

My attention was torn.

After she'd identified the photographs of her children, I had asked Mrs. Campbell whether she had any family who could come and stay with her, which had elicited the information that she had a sister who also lived in Inverness. I'd made the telephone call myself, after Mrs. Campbell had given me her sister's number, and then I'd sat with her for nearly an hour while we waited for her sister to arrive.

Even second-hand grief was draining—all the more so because I hadn't been able to help Mrs. Campbell, and yet I couldn't think of anything else that I could have done for her.

Even that memory, though, was troubling me less than the fact that Flynn and Becky still hadn't returned to the inn when I'd gone back there myself around supper time.

The maid who cleaned our rooms said that she'd seen them come in briefly, then leave again, dressed in hiking gear, and the girl at the receptionist's desk said that they'd asked directions for getting to Urquhart Castle—none of which reassured me in the slightest. Although at least I had a place to start searching if they weren't back when I returned to the Inn.

The clock now read ten minutes to midnight, and I was inclined to agree with Violet. If Preston were coming, he would have been here by now.

"Do you think he was lying?" I asked. "That he never intended to meet us here at all?"

"I hope so." Violet's mouth twisted briefly as she said it. "I never thought I'd say those words—that I'm hoping that Preston is just being his usually thoroughly aggravating self. Because the alternative …"

She stopped, shaking her head.

Neither of us had to put the alternative into words. If Preston had been following a lead on Urquhart, we could both imagine all too clearly what could have happened to him. After her experience being kidnapped, drugged, and nearly drowned, no doubt Violet could visualise the possible ways for Preston's mission to go wrong in even more painful detail than I could.

"Is there anything in the newspaper about the London bombing?" Violet asked.

To pass the time—and to distract myself from worrying about Flynn and Becky—I had been glancing through a copy of the London *Times* that another patron had left on the table.

"Not that I've seen," I told her. "But there's quite a nice fiery editorial all about how there's an epidemic of disease threatening men, women, and children alike, and yet the government is wasting money and lives on a conquest against the Boers in South Africa."

"That's more or less what Mr. Holmes was expecting, isn't it," Violet said.

"It is."

"I wonder whether he's thought of tracking down the authors of these newspaper pieces?"

"Knowing Holmes, I'm sure he has." No doubt he and Watson would be finding out all they could about the sources behind the newspaper reporters' stories. And Jack would be working with Lestrade and Gregson to investigate any possible leads on Blinder—

"You're thinking about your husband, aren't you?"

Violet's question interrupted my train of thought and made me look up.

"Yes. How did you know?" I wasn't used to anyone but Jack and Holmes being able to read my thoughts with any degree of accuracy.

Violet shrugged. "My father was a drunk. What you'd call a mean drunk. He died in a barroom brawl, but before that, I grew up constantly watching him for any sign that he was going to snap and fly into one of his rages."

"I'm sorry."

She shrugged again. "Ironically, it was excellent training for a career in detective work—all that practice in reading even the most minute changes in people's facial expressions." She refocused on me. "Your husband must be quite extraordinary. Letting you come up here alone to pursue a criminal investigation."

"Extraordinary, yes. But Jack doesn't *let* me do anything—any more than I *let* him go to work at Scotland Yard."

Violet studied me, and for a moment, she seemed on the verge of saying something more. But then she stood up abruptly.

"Preston isn't coming," she said. "We might as well go back to the Inn."

Chapter 33: Watson

"Is it something in the water, doctor?"

The man spoke in a hoarse whisper. The whites of his dark eyes bulged in their sunken sockets. The skin on his face hung flaccid and wrinkled, signs of severe dehydration. His bluish skin was another sign of a circulatory system dangerously close to failure.

There were eleven more men like him in the ward at St. Thomas Hospital. There had been thirteen patients this morning. It was now two o'clock and two of the beds were empty, their former occupants having died.

"We don't know the cause as yet," I said.

"They say there's something in the water," he continued. "But the nurses here are making me drink it. I'm just getting so weak …" His voice trailed off.

We were in a third-floor wing at St. Thomas's, three floors above the laboratory where Holmes and I had nearly met death from the clockwork dynamite bomb four days earlier.

St. Thomas had been selected as the central gathering point for patients, primarily for its size and the ability to control access from the public.

"Is it cholera?" the man asked.

I wanted to be reassuring. I wanted to tell the truth as well.

"We believe it may be. We are not certain. We have taken

samples from all the patients and the laboratory is preparing slides for microscopic—"

I broke off. The patient had suddenly convulsed. I called for the nurse, and grasped him by the shoulders, leaning forward to steady him, watching his mouth in case he should swallow his tongue. The convulsion subsided. Fortunately, he was still breathing.

Along with dehydration, convulsions were also symptoms associated with cholera. I had seen men die of the disease in Bombay, when I had just arrived for the tour of duty that would soon take me to Afghanistan. But there, sanitary conditions could be appallingly inadequate.

Here in London, there had not been a cholera outbreak for nearly thirty years. Till now, Londoners had been proud and confident in our modern purification system, of which the Hampton Works was a part. The various components drew water from upstream in the Thames, filtered it, and sent it to reservoirs, and then piped it to the London population.

Extensive samples had been taken from the Hampton Works and its reservoirs. From those samples, no trace of the comma-shaped cholera bacillus had yet been spotted on a microscope slide.

Yet, now in London were eleven patients exhibiting all the signs of the disease.

There was an antidote for cholera, being developed in Germany, I had been told. But it was not ready.

Aloud I said, "You are getting the best treatment we have at the moment."

The nurse appeared, with her bright smile and starched white cap and collar, bearing a water pitcher.

"Hydration," she said, and filled a water glass. "Drink it up for me, there's a good gentleman."

The patient drank a few sips and turned his face away. "I'm just so tired," he said.

Mercifully, his convulsion had lasted less than one minute. The two patients who had died this morning had convulsed progressively longer and more frequently, as their bodies struggled to expel the disease.

"You may be able to help us," I said, after the nurse had gone. "If you can describe your movements prior to the time you were taken ill."

He pointed a trembling finger to the chart at the foot of his bed. "I told the nurse. She wrote it down."

I picked up the chart. I read. The patient was a banker, living and working in Westminster. Saturday, the day before he had taken ill, he had taken supper at the Savoy prior to seeing a play.

"The chart says you dined at the Savoy. Do you recall what you ate?"

He shook his head. "Everything is so hazy."

"Were there others at your table?"

"My wife and another couple. We all had the whitefish."

"And they were not taken ill?"

"Only me."

I wondered. Could this be a hitherto-unknown strain of the disease that only affected certain people? And was undetectable by a microscope? It seemed preposterous.

I asked the nurse to bring me the charts of the other patients, including the charts of the two men who had died. I took a blank page from one of the charts and wrote out the names of more restaurants, and more theatrical performances the unfortunate men had attended. No two were the same.

"I'm going to die, aren't I?" the man asked.

"Keep drinking water, my friend," I said. "You must help your body wash away the disease."

Chapter 34: Watson

On my way out from the hospital, I made the mistake of exiting through the main lobby. Two Metropolitan Police constables were guarding the entrance.

I recognised one of them, a friend of Jack Kelly's. "Those are reporters outside, sir. You may want to take another exit."

I made another mistake and pressed forward. A moment later I found myself accosted by a flurry of shouted questions.

"It's Doctor Watson!"

"Look, the initials are on his medical bag!"

"Can you confirm the shocking conditions in the water system?"

"Is a deadly disease breeding in the neglected pipes?"

"Is it true the laboratory tests are false?"

"The administration hiding the truth?"

"Will Sherlock Holmes expose them?"

I made the mistake of responding.

"You had best stay away from me," I said. "If I am contagious. It is only fair to warn you."

"Have you infected Sherlock Holmes?"

I turned on my heel and I walked back into the hospital. The bronze statue of Queen Victoria seemed to reproach me. I took a side exit to the street, where I hailed a passing cab.

"Baker Street," I said.

Chapter 35: Watson

I entered our sitting room to find that Holmes had spread out a large map of London onto our table. At the top of the map was a leather-trimmed box.

"Well?" he asked.

I reported.

He listened in silence, pausing only to ask if I had listed the restaurants visited by the unfortunate patients I had seen in the hospital.

I handed him the page on which I had written out the names.

"Excellent," he said, and opened the leather-trimmed box. I saw a set of ivory chess pieces.

Within two minutes he had carefully placed pawns on the map locations corresponding to the restaurants I had listed. Then he stepped back.

"Examine this map, Watson," he said. "What can we learn from these locations?"

I considered. Thirteen pawns were arranged in a cluster covering perhaps a dozen blocks.

"All in Covent Garden," I said.

"The theatre district," Holmes said. "All dined there Saturday."

"Before a performance," I said. "But not all went to the same performance."

"What does that tell us?"

"I do not know."

"Come, Watson. What did those pamphlets say? What did those reporters say?"

"That the water supply was contaminated with a new strain of cholera."

"And is that possible, given what we know of the patients who have the disease?"

"I cannot imagine how cholera could be in the water of a restaurant with only one person becoming infected."

"So, what do we have, if we eliminate that impossibility?"

"The disease is not in the water supply."

He gave me a long look. "Yes, and so what possibility remains?"

"That someone intends the public to *think* that the disease is in the water supply."

"And how did that someone accomplish that deception?"

I shrugged.

"Let me add one more piece of evidence," he said. He took a telegraph message from his pocket. "This wire is from the Koch Institute in Berlin. It affirms that they have been working on an antidote for cholera, and to that end have succeeded in isolating the bacillus for reproduction and testing purposes. Moreover, it confirms that a portion of the isolated bacteria solution went missing some three days ago."

Suddenly my imagination produced an image. "A small vial," I said. "With the stolen cholera. A person could go from restaurant to restaurant. A busy Saturday night. He discreetly walks past a table. Perhaps he has an eyedropper. A few drops in a drinking glass here or there …"

I spread my palms.

Holmes gave one of his tight smiles. "Would that the solution were so apparent. But there are two difficulties. First, how did the stolen bacteria solution get from Berlin in time to be utilised on Saturday night?"

I was not deterred. "The theft was not noticed till Saturday. But it could have taken place many days previously."

"Very well. We will pass on to the second difficulty. How do you account for the absence of cholera in any of the blood samples taken from the patients at St. Thomas Hospital?"

I thought for a long moment. "Perhaps the extraction and isolation process has altered the bacillus in some way."

Holmes did not look convinced. But at that moment came a ring from our bell-pull. I recognised Mrs. Hudson's voice and then Gregson's.

"Let us hear the inspector's news before we continue," Holmes said.

Soon Gregson was with us in our sitting-room.

A dejected frown clouded his Nordic features.

"What news, Inspector?"

"It's another dead end, I'm afraid," he said. "The Royal Navy sighted the *Avenger*, Blinder's yacht. She was in the North Channel waters, headed Northeast."

"North*east*?" I asked. "Not towards Scotland?"

"Towards Amsterdam," Gregson said. "At least, that was the seaport nearest to where the *Avenger* was sighted."

"So Blinder and Inverness may not be connected after all," I said. "Or perhaps he has changed his plan—"

Holmes held up his hand. He appeared to be listening to Mrs. Hudson, downstairs. She was speaking to someone in the hallway. A moment later the front door closed, and I heard our landlady's footsteps on the stairs.

She opened our sitting-room door.

"A wire from Becky, Mr. Holmes," she said.

"Becky?" I asked.

Holmes tore open the yellow envelope.

He glanced at the message and passed it over to Gregson.

"Another dead end," Gregson said, handing the message to me.

"On the contrary," said Holmes. "It means we must notify Jack immediately."

"Jack Kelly? Why?"

"The four of us must take the next train for Inverness."

CHAPTER 36: BECKY

"So that's Urquhart Castle," Flynn said.

"That's the place," Becky agreed. She was trying not to shiver.

Urquhart Castle stood on a rocky outcropping overlooking Loch Ness at its narrowest southern point. There was a red sunset tonight, which showed up the eerie ruins of the tumbled-down castle walls, and the black, bottomless-looking expanse of water beyond.

However hard Becky tried not to, she kept thinking about every ghost story she'd ever read, every legend she'd ever heard of castles haunted by the headless spectres of their former lords.

"According to the guidebook, the Scots and English kept fighting for control of the castle during the Wars of Independence. Then during the Jacobite Risings, the last of the government troops garrisoned here blew up the castle when they left."

It was too dark for her to read the guidebook now, even by the setting sunlight, but she'd memorised the entry on Urquhart Castle on the ride here. They'd hired a cab at the train station and paid the cabman to drive them out to the Loch, and he'd agreed only because they'd assured him that he wouldn't have to wait for them.

Right now, Becky was wishing that they'd tried offering him more money to stay and drive them back to the Inn when they were finished.

"Did the guidebook have anything to say about sea monsters?" Flynn asked.

He didn't seem to find anything frightening or uncanny about the deserted ruin before them. He'd already started scrambling over the low, tumbled-down stones of the castle's outer walls, heading for the edge of the Loch.

Becky followed, boosting herself up and scrambling to the top of a low wall. "Just an old story about a monk. Whoever wrote the guidebook says that it was probably a catfish or an eel."

She jumped down off the wall, landing with a thump on the other side.

The noise must have disturbed a nest of bats roosting in the ruined walls, because a group of the creatures burst out of the ruined castle keep and flapped around on leathery wings, making Becky jump. An owl hooted softly from somewhere close by.

Flynn hopped over another wall without pausing or sparing the bats more than a passing glance.

Ordinarily, Becky would sooner have run a mile over hot coals than admit to being frightened, but she couldn't stop herself from giving him an incredulous look.

"You don't think there's anything … creepy about this place?"

"Creepy?" Flynn looked at her over his shoulder. "Nah, there's no one around. Not a soul." He gestured to the deserted expanse of ruins and the black, shadowy Loch beyond. "So, what's going to happen? We get eaten by a sea monster? We both know there's no such thing."

He was right. Becky knew he was right, but she still shivered again and looked back over her shoulder as they climbed up the hill on which the ruined castle stood. The sun had now sunk below the horizon, but the moon was up, casting a silver trail as they finally stood at the base of the broken-down castle tower. Leaning against one of the stone walls, Becky caught her breath, turning to look back the way that they had come.

Flynn was probably right that they were alone out here, but after their encounter with Urquhart, she couldn't shake the nasty feeling that they were being followed.

Flynn was looking out over the Loch when he said, sharply, "What's that?"

"Very funny," Becky said without turning around. "But you can just give up on trying to scare me by pretending to see something in the water. We agreed that there's no such thing as sea monsters."

"Yeah. Well, maybe." Flynn's voice had an odd note in it, one she'd only rarely heard from him before, and it made her turn around to look at him. He was standing right on the edge of the rocky promontory, staring down into the water below. "But I think that thing"—he pointed downwards—"would have a different opinion."

Becky almost accused him of trying to scare her again, but his eyes were wide enough that she stepped forwards, joining him in looking down into the Loch.

A huge, monstrous head rose from out of the moonlit water, supported by a slender serpent's neck. Behind it rose the hump of a massive body.

The creature glided noiselessly through the water, propelling itself deeper into the Loch.

"What—" Becky's voice came out in a whisper.

"I don't know," Flynn said. "But that's definitely no eel."

CHAPTER 37: WATSON

We were clattering northward in a first-class carriage on the Highland Express train, bound for Inverness. Jack had come directly from Scotland Yard to meet us at Euston Station. Gregson was at Jack's side, across from Holmes and me.

Jack leaned forward, his dark eyes intense and glittering. "Glad I got here in time. How much danger is Lucy in?"

For answer, Holmes handed Jack the telegram we had received in Baker Street.

"From Becky."

"Becky? Sending a telegram on her own?"

"It may be Lucy, using a different name. The language is guarded, as you will see."

"She thinks they're being watched."

"Assuredly they are," Holmes said. "I would wish them to be together, the four of them, but we surrendered control when we let them go off on their own."

"They have come through other dangers," I said.

"Would you please read the telegram aloud," Holmes said.

Jack did so.

> "Strathmore Hotel, Inverness. Monday 9 AM. L and V not yet connected to P. Some reports of strange activity at Urquhart Castle, which F and I will investigate today. Urquhart's shop

sells tonics and herbs and remedies. They make their own castor oil from the beans. U is on hand and looking for us. R. Kelly."

"Was it 'U'—meaning 'Urquhart'—is on hand' that made this so urgent?" Jack asked, handing back the yellow paper.

Holmes shook his head. "We expected him to be there in Inverness. What makes this urgent is the extra information Becky provides: namely, that the company manufactures their own castor oil," Holmes said.

"I'm still puzzled."

"Castor oil is made by pressing castor beans to expel the oil. The remaining pulp is mildly toxic, and so revolting in taste and smell that it is unlikely to be ingested. However, alcohol may be utilised to extract the poisonous element from the crushed bean residue. From the resulting solution, a deadly poison may be readily precipitated. It is called ricin, and the ingestion of only a few grains—less than a pinch of salt—is lethal."

Jack pointed to the telegram. "Becky knows that?"

"She does, as does Flynn. We have discussed it."

"So, Urquhart has the raw materials to make this deadly poison."

"His shop has been manufacturing castor oil for quite some time."

"Was that what killed the three people in Whitehall?" asked Gregson.

"The three victims each had a puncture mark below the ear, close to the jugular vein. That would be an effective pathway into which to introduce the poison, which would have caused death within a few hours. Likely they were given a mild sedative first to make them more tractable to accept the injection. Or an alcoholic drink. Whisky, perhaps. The lack of test evidence from the autopsy, ironically, could in fact indicate the presence of ricin, since that is one of the poisons not susceptible to a confirmation test."

"What about the patients in St. Thomas Hospital?"

"Those I saw," I said, "had the symptoms of cholera. Convulsions, fluid on the lungs, internal organ failure—"

"Which symptoms are identical to ricin poisoning," Holmes said.

"And can be trumpeted in the newspapers as cholera."

"So, the idea that the London water supply is contaminated due to neglect of the water system—that's all a blind," Jack said.

"And a most effective one, given the actual occurrence of acute sickness and death," Holmes said. "To achieve the desired state of public alarm and consequent hostility towards the incumbent government, only a few persons need come down with the symptoms. The newspapers will fan the flames."

I remembered my original idea about someone spreading the cholera bacillus. That method, as Holmes had pointed out at the time, would not have been consistent with the facts. But I saw now that, with ricin instead of cholera, all obstacles to the method I had first envisioned would be overcome.

I spoke up. "The hospital patients that I saw were all taken ill after dining out. Someone with a small phial of ricin might readily travel from restaurant to restaurant, or tea room to tea room, wherever the public gathers. Hover behind a waiter, heavily laden with his tray, wait for him to set down the tray and serve the first guest. When his back is turned, pass by and sprinkle a few grains of the toxin onto one of the remaining plates. Or into a water glass."

"The poison has a bitter taste," Holmes said. "Care would be needed in the placement."

"In such a small amount it might not be noticed. Only few grains—"

"It might be pressed into tiny tablets and inserted into a salt cellar," said Gregson.

"The devilish cunning of it all is that not every attempt needs to succeed," Jack said. "The newspapers can fan the flames, as you pointed out."

"The selection of victims seen by Dr. Watson is also instructive regarding the intentions of the poisoners."

"In what way?" Gregson asked.

"The patients I saw at St. Thomas's were all relatively well-off," I responded. "And all male."

"Voters," Gregson said.

"The election," Jack said. "That was the commissioner's fear, and Mycroft's too, that the election would be manipulated. Someone is doing just that. And if that someone is Blinder, he now has another million dollars in stolen bearer bonds to invest in the plot."

"I saw the patient records myself," Holmes said. "I telephoned Mycroft before we left Baker Street. Mycroft promises that a Royal Navy destroyer will be anchored in Inverness Harbour when we arrive."

"What good will that do?" Jack asked.

"We shall have to wait and see," Holmes replied.

CHAPTER 38: LUCY

"A sea monster," I repeated.

Violet and I were seated in the inn's small breakfast room which was—thankfully—deserted at the moment apart from ourselves. I had slept the night before, but not until late, when Flynn and Becky had returned to the inn and were both safely in their beds, asleep.

Violet didn't look as though she had slept at all. She wore the same tweed skirt and white blouse she'd had on yesterday, both rumpled, as though she'd never taken them off and had simply lain down in her clothes. Her eyes were puffy and shadowed, and she'd tapped on my door at half-past five o'clock to ask whether I'd heard any news.

Morning sunlight filtered through the lace curtains at the window. Our table was spread with toast and marmalade and bowls of porridge, although neither Violet nor I had much of an appetite.

The telegram that had arrived for me from London lay by the cup of coffee I'd just set down when Flynn and Becky had come clattering down the stairs. Although I'd have preferred to be fortified with the entire pot's worth of coffee before I had to cope with the story that Flynn and Becky were jostling and interrupting each other to tell.

Becky gestured impatiently. "Something that *looked* like a sea monster, I said. We both saw it." She glanced at Flynn for confirmation, who nodded.

"Had a long neck like a snake and a body a bit like a whale."

"And it wasn't just a dummy or a model," Becky added. "Because it swam—or at least, it moved. Quickly, too. About as fast as a strong man could row a boat, or maybe even faster."

"And you saw it in the water below Urquhart Castle?"

Flynn and Becky bobbed their heads in simultaneous agreement.

"All right, then." I took one last sip of coffee before standing up. "It sounds as though we have today's program already decided for us: a sightseeing trip to Urquhart Castle. We can decide whether we want to split up once we get there. A trip by boat around the Loch might be useful, too, to see whether you can spot any evidence that the supposed monster may have left behind last night."

Flynn nodded. "I saw a sign yesterday advertising boating tours."

"Good, then we'll do that first."

Violet hadn't spoken at all while Flynn and Becky were telling their story, but now she opened her mouth to utter a single word.

"Preston?"

Her voice was calm and so was her expression. But her fingers were gripping the handle of the teacup so tightly that her knuckles stood out white.

How she felt about Preston was none of my business.

So I said, only, "I'm sorry. I know it's not a good sign that he never turned up at McGregor's last night. Ordinarily, I'd suggest visiting all the likely inns and guest houses in Inverness to see whether we can find out where he was staying and when he was last seen. But as it is ... investigating Urquhart and Blinder and whatever operation they're running here is probably our best lead in investigating his disappearance, too. Find them and we're likely to find him."

Or at least, find out what had happened to him. I didn't say that out loud, but I was sure Violet knew as well as I did that it was by no means a given that Preston was still alive.

Violet swallowed, but nodded. "I know. You're right."

Flynn and Becky exchanged a look—the kind of look that said I was definitely going to wish I'd had more coffee before they'd finished whatever they were about to say.

"What is it?" I asked.

Flynn scuffed his shoe against the floor. Becky fiddled with the buttons on her dress.

"The thing to remember is that we're fine," she said. "Neither of us got hurt at all."

"Oh good. I love stories that come with that kind of preamble." I sighed. "Let me guess. You saw either Blinder or Urquhart yesterday and were nearly captured but got away again?"

"More or less." Becky studied my face warily, clearly trying to decide just how much trouble she was going to get into by telling me the full story.

"It's all right," I told her. "Since you're both here, I'll assume that you were fully capable of handling whatever predicament you got yourselves into. So, you can tell me all about it on the way to the Loch. But first I need to leave a message for Holmes."

Becky and Flynn both stared. "Holmes?"

"Yes." I gestured to the opened telegram on the table. "I've just had word from him this morning. He, Watson, Gregson, and Jack are on their way to Scotland."

Chapter 39: Watson

"They left just after they took breakfast." Mr. Clark, the manager of the Strathmore Inn, gave a cooperative smile from behind his carved-oak reception desk. "She and her two children, and their nanny."

Holmes looked up from his examination of the hotel register. "Did she leave a message?"

Jack and Gregson were outside, a few doors down the block, checking in at the local police station prior to hiring a boat to take us to Urquhart Castle. The time was just after ten in the morning. We had arrived at Inverness Station less than a half-hour ago, and I was looking forward to a substantial breakfast, or at least a strong coffee.

"I believe there was a message for a Mr. Holmes." The clerk rummaged in his desk drawer. Then he shook his head. "Now, Gladys," he called to a woman tidying up the small hotel parlour, "what did you do with that envelope we had from the nice young lady?"

The woman looked up, dust cloth in her hand, eyes wide and mouth open.

"Why, I give it to that Mr. Holmes," she said.

Holmes looked up from the registrar with some interest. "I am Mr. Holmes," he said.

"I can attest to that," I said.

"If you say so." The woman put down her dust cloth and came over to join us. "But how was I to know? Fellow looked perfectly ordinary and respectable too—"

"Never mind," said Holmes. Surprisingly, he appeared completely disinterested in the matter. "No harm done. Probably a mistake of some kind. Now, my four associates and I should like accommodations for the night. Can you fit us all in?"

The clerk's expression changed from worried to eagerly forthcoming as he saw the bank note Holmes held between his thumb and fingertips. "Let me just consult the registry," he said. He did so and looked up, smiling. "One night only, is that correct? Then yes, we can. Four persons. Four rooms. The bath is down the hall. Second floor."

"If you can just give me one of the keys," Holmes said, handing the note to Mr. Clark. "Watson, can you please give the other two keys to our two companions who are waiting outside? Mr. Clark, would you please be good enough to have coffee and biscuits for four sent up to my room?"

"I'll see to it," Clark said.

He left for the kitchen. The parlour maid remained.

"And you, madam?" Holmes turned to her. "Would you please go outside with Dr. Watson and hold the door for him when he comes in? He will be retrieving our luggage from the porch."

She went to the front door. I followed her outside.

Jack and Gregson were nowhere to be seen, of course, and neither were our suitcases, for we had already left them at the Fenton hotel, across the street.

Doing my best to appear embarrassed, I said, "They're not here, and neither is our luggage. I can't think what might have happened to them."

"Gone over to the Fenton, I expect," she said. Indicating the hotel and coffee shop. "We lose a lot o' room nights to the Fenton."

"Well, I'll just have to wait here," I said. "I'll discuss it with Mr. Holmes."

I took my key and walked up two flights of stairs. My room was 27. I had two more keys, 26 and 25. Number 28, I deduced, was Holmes's.

That door was locked. I rapped, but Holmes did not answer.

I was wondering what to do when the door opened on the stairwell and Holmes appeared.

"Where were you?" I asked.

"Lucy's room. I saw the number in the register and obtained her key when the staff was otherwise engaged." He tapped his coat pocket. "She left a message."

Chapter 40: Flynn

Flynn wasn't sure how he felt about being out on a boat again, so soon after almost drowning in the Thames.

He wouldn't go so far as to say he was afraid, but he'd have preferred to be standing on solid ground. The waters of the Loch looked smooth, but the small sail boat that they'd rented for an hour's cruise still kept tipping and rolling unpleasantly, buffeted by the wind.

The boatman wasn't helping, either. An old, grey-haired man with a face like seamed wood, he kept coming out with helpful facts about Loch Ness, raising his voice to be heard above the wind.

"Seven hundred feet deep in places. It's peat from the soil all around that gives the water the dark colour." He chuckled. "Fall in, and our Loch monster could have you in its mouth before you ever saw it coming."

Miss Violet was looking a bit green. Maybe she was thinking about their escape from Blinder's sinking boat, too.

Lucy was seated nearby the boat pilot at the tiller. She at least didn't look bothered. She was holding her hat on with one hand, smiling and looking interested while she listened to the pilot.

Lucy was very good at getting people to talk.

"Oh, but surely you don't believe that about a Loch Monster?" she asked. "We thought it was just a legend."

"Oh aye." Despite what he said, Flynn thought the pilot looked a bit uncomfortable. "Just a joke, ma'am. Just a bit o' fun, that's all."

Lucy let it go, pointing up ahead. "And is that Urquhart Castle? What a beautiful, picturesque old place! Could you get us any closer? I'd love to see the ruins from the water."

If anything, the pilot looked even more uncomfortable than before. "Sorry, ma'am, I can't do that. There's ... there's rocks under that outcropping the castle stands on. Might tear a hole in the hull of the boat."

"Oh, but surely that's an underground waterway I can see just below the castle?" Lucy gave the pilot a look of wide-eyed innocence and pointed. "Ships must have been able to go in there at one time?"

"Well, yes." The pilot coughed and made a sound like *harrumph*. "The water gate. I believe they used to bring supplies into the castle that way. Verra' useful, when the place was under siege. But there was a rock fall ... oh, a while back. It's no' safe anymore." He swung the tiller, turning the boat around. "Now, we must be headin' back to the dock, but I'll show you some other nice spots on the way."

* * *

Half an hour later, they were all standing on the boat dock, watching their pilot steer another group of holiday sightseers out onto the Loch.

Miss Violet was the one to say what they were all thinking. "He didn't at all like us asking about Urquhart Castle or the underground waterway, did he?"

"No, he definitely did not," Lucy agreed. She tilted her head, looking up at the sky. "It's afternoon now. I was going to suggest that we visit Urquhart Castle, but now I think maybe we ought to delay that pleasure for a few more hours."

"Until after dark, you mean?" Flynn asked.

"Exactly."

"I think we should split up," Becky said. "You and Violet can look around the ruins. Flynn and I will see whether there's anything to be seen in the waterway under the castle. We can probably find a rowboat to steal—I mean, borrow. I saw a few on the docks we passed on the boat tour."

Lucy hesitated. Flynn could tell she wasn't keen on the idea of letting them go off alone.

"We'll be safer than you would be," Becky said. "If someone sees us, we're just a couple of children who got separated from our governess on a family picnic. You'd be suspicious if you went climbing around underground tunnels, but children do that kind of thing all the time."

Flynn could tell from Lucy's expression that she knew Becky was right. "We'll wait until nightfall," Lucy said. "Then find our way up to the castle separately, just in case anyone is watching. We don't want anyone to see us arrive together." She glanced at Violet. "How do you feel about a tour of the countryside on horseback?"

Violet grimaced. "I suppose it has to be better than a boat."

"All right then." Lucy refocused on Becky and Flynn. "Just promise me that you'll be careful. And if you see anything—any sign at all of danger—turn around and come find Violet and me."

Becky nodded. "We will. Promise."

Chapter 41: Becky

"Why don't we ever get to investigate nice, bright happy places?" Becky whispered.

She and Flynn had left their borrowed rowboat anchored in the waterway under the castle, and were picking their way along a narrow stone passage. It was pitch black, so dark that she couldn't even see Flynn's outline in the passage ahead of her, and they had to rely completely on touch. The air was dank and chilly, and every time Becky's hand brushed against one of the stone walls, it came away feeling slimy.

"Right," Flynn muttered back. "Next crime we investigate has to take place in a circus. I'll make a note of it now."

Actually, they had investigated a murder inside a circus once. Becky had to admit that it hadn't really been any better.

A very faint, very distant, but rhythmic sound reached her ears. "Do you hear that?" she whispered.

"No, but if you keep talking, someone'll probably hear us and come to investigate—" Flynn stopped mid-sentence and halted, so abruptly that Becky walked straight into him, nearly knocking them both over.

"Now who's making a commotion?" she hissed. "You could give me a warning next time."

She sensed rather than saw Flynn hold up a hand. "Is that what you heard?"

Becky listened and heard the sound again. "That's it. What is it, do you think?"

"Sounds like a generator engine—for electricity," Flynn murmured back. "Come on, let's keep going—and keep quiet."

"Oh, well, I was going to start playing a trumpet and crashing cymbals together, but if you think we should be quiet—"

Becky followed Flynn, creeping along the passage and trying to step carefully to avoid making any noise. Now and then a loose stone or piece of rubble rolled under her foot, and she didn't want to kick anything that would go clattering off into the dark.

"There's a light up ahead." Flynn's voice had dropped to a near soundless murmur. He'd stopped walking again, but this time there was enough of a glow that Becky was able to see him and stop in time.

It wasn't really a light, but further up the passageway, the darkness grew less penetrating, softening from pitch black to charcoal grey. As they crept closer, Becky saw that the passageway ended in a big wooden door, with faint shafts of light filtering from around the edges. The steady, rhythmic drive of the engine was louder, now, definitely coming from somewhere behind the door.

Becky listened for a long moment. On the bright side, the engine was loud enough that no one was likely to hear any noise they made out here. But they still had to decide how likely they were to find Urquhart, Blinder, or another guard directly on the other side of the door.

"Do we risk going in?" she whispered.

"Rule number one of any good sneak thief," Flynn whispered back.

"What's that?"

"Never risk opening a door when you can get a look through the key hole first."

He dropped to crouch down in front of the door, peering through the metal hole in the lock plate, which was big enough that it must have been fashioned for the type of huge, old-fashioned keys that medieval ladies wore on their belts in paintings.

He was there for so long that Becky finally asked, "Well?"

Wordlessly, Flynn got to his feet and stepped aside so that she could have a chance to peer through. Becky bent to put her eye to the key hole, drawing in a quick breath at what she saw.

The space inside was like a huge, circular cavern, with a domed roof overhead. The generator they could hear running was apparently producing electricity—enough for hundreds of electric lights strung up on chains across the ceiling. Weird shadows danced and flickered across the walls.

A huge vat loomed in the centre of the room, heated by a glowing fire that seemed to be fuelled by some kind of big metal cylinder with tubes attached.

Becky glanced up at Flynn. "What is that big metal thing?"

"A tank of coal gas. That'd be my guess, anyway. Mr. Holmes showed me a picture of factory workers using compressed coal gas to keep fires going."

This was definitely a factory operation of some kind.

A platform supported by levels of metal scaffolding rose above the vat, while at the bottom were rows of small spigots, like the ones Becky had seen pub owners use to draw beer on tap.

Workers dressed in white coveralls and hair nets were lined up, opening and closing the small spigots to let liquid pour from the vat into glass bottles. Then they would cork the bottles and carry them over to a long table, where more workers would paste brightly coloured labels onto the glass sides before putting the bottles into wooden crates.

"What's on the labels, can you see?" Flynn whispered.

"I can't read the words, we're not close enough," Becky answered back. "But I'd bet that they say it's a health tonic or something like that. The bottles in Urquhart's pharmacy had labels that looked just the same."

"Health tonic." Flynn snorted. "First health tonic I've ever seen that needs armed guards."

"I know."

Becky had noted the men, too, lined up against one wall and watching the workers who were filling the bottles. There were four of them, all dressed in dark clothing and with rifles slung over their shoulders.

As Becky pressed her eye to the key hole again, she saw one woman stumble a bit on her way from carrying a newly filled bottle over to the labelling station.

Instantly, the guards tensed, and one of them barked, "Be careful with that! No spilling, remember, or the cost comes out of your wages."

Becky watched the woman flinch and scuttle away, carefully balancing the tonic bottle between her two hands.

"I wonder whether they actually believe they're producing a health tonic."

Flynn shrugged. "Pay people enough and most of them won't ask too many inconvenient questions."

He gestured for Becky to move over and then crouched down, looking through into the cavernous room again.

"Do you need all that equipment to produce ricin?" he asked.

"I don't know. I can't remember enough of what Mr. Holmes told us about its production," Becky said. "I don't know why they'd need bottles and bottles of it, either, unless they're planning to poison an entire city. But I'd bet any odds that ricin is involved here somehow."

Flynn started to answer, then stopped, raising his head alertly. "Did you hear something?"

Becky listened, too, straining to hear over the continued steady chug-chug of the generator.

"Someone ... moaning?"

Flynn nodded. "Either this place really is haunted, or else there's someone here."

"Where are they, though?"

The intermittent moaning was faint and echoed weirdly in the narrow stone confines of the passage so that Becky had a hard time guessing where the sound was coming from.

Flynn listened, as well, and finally said, "Somewhere back that way?" he pointed along the passage the way that they had come from the underground waterway.

"Did we pass by any other rooms or passageways?" Becky asked.

"We could have passed fifty of them and never noticed in the dark. The question is whether we want to see who's groaning or go find Miss Violet and Lucy first."

Becky had to admit that the second option was tempting. The cold, dank atmosphere alone was raising goose bumps all up and down her arms, and that wasn't even taking into consideration all the guards with guns inside the factory chamber, and the possibility that Urquhart and Blinder could be somewhere around.

But she shook her head. "What if we leave and can't get back in here without being seen? We'd better find out who it is for ourselves while we have the chance."

She bent and took one last look in at the vat and the factory workers, but the operations were continuing without any more hitches or pauses. Definitely no sign that anyone was likely to come out of the door and down the passage any time soon.

"Let's go."

She and Flynn crept along the narrow tunnel, keeping their hands outstretched to feel for doorways or branches in the passage and straining their ears to listen for any more sounds.

After a minute or two of complete silence save for the quiet rasp of their own breathing, Becky was beginning to wonder whether they'd just imagined the noise. But then it came again: a low, wordless groan.

Becky had heard that kind of noise before. It was the sound men made when they'd been knocked unconscious and were beginning to come around.

They'd come far enough from the doorway that the darkness was once more complete, like having your face muffled in black fabric. Becky couldn't see Flynn at all, but she whispered, "I think that came from somewhere off on your side of the tunnel."

She heard the rustle of Flynn reaching out and groping in the darkness, silence, more rustles, and then Flynn said, "There's an entrance to another passage here. Careful, you want to duck your head. It's a lot lower than this one."

He was right. No wonder that they hadn't noticed the branch in the tunnel the first time they'd passed by it. The ceiling was so low that Becky had to bend almost double in order to get through, and it was still inky dark. She shuffled along behind Flynn, trying to stretch out her hands in front so that she wouldn't brain herself if the ceiling dropped any lower.

"Keep going. It opens up a bit ahead," Flynn said.

Becky groped her way forward and felt the tunnel walls end in what seemed to be the entrance to a bigger room.

She straightened up. "Where are we?"

"Search me." Flynn must have reached into his pocket for a match, because the next moment a small light flared in the darkness, giving Becky a quick glimpse of the room around them: walls, floor, and ceiling all built of the same grey stone.

She was about to hiss at Flynn that they'd better put the light out before someone saw, when she caught sight of something on the far wall.

"Over there—hurry!" She pointed.

Flynn followed her, although halfway across his match burned down to his fingers and he had to drop it and light another. They reached the far wall, and the second match's faint glow was enough to show the heavy metal grate set into the wall, blocking off a small, windowless section of the room.

Flynn's mouth pursed in a silent whistle. "Looks like a prison cell."

"It doesn't just look like one. See there?" Becky pointed to a man's figure lying sprawled in a corner of the cell on the stone floor. The second match burned out, too, but not before they were able to see the man's face. "It's hard to tell, but I think it might be Preston."

CHAPTER 42: WATSON

The boat that Jack and Gregson had arranged for us was a harbour tender, a small wooden vessel resembling a lightweight tugboat, used to bring passengers or light cargo from the Inverness docks to the ships moored further out. She was steam-powered, similar to those I had seen on the Thames, but with limited engine capacity.

She badly needed paint.

"The best you could do?" asked Holmes.

"Not much available," Jack said. "We asked our friends at the police station, and they say the captain's reputable. Knows the Loch. By the way, we saw Blinder's yacht, the *Avenger*, coming into the Inverness Harbour. A Royal Navy destroyer is anchored a hundred yards out. They can't help but see it go by."

"The name of the destroyer?"

"HMS *Daring*," Jack replied. "Why?"

"I expect Mycroft arranged that. Her captain was particularly helpful to us in the Adam Worth matter five years ago."

I remembered the case. The weight of my old service handgun gave a comforting heft to my coat pocket.

Holmes took a step backwards and nodded to Jack to come closer. He lowered his voice.

Gregson was up front, conversing with the captain, a rustic old fellow whose florid cheeks and thick grey hair bespoke an active life on the local waters.

"Lucy left me a message," Holmes said. "In addition to the one at the front desk."

"The one that was stolen," Jack said. With a note of pride, he added, "She must have anticipated that." Holmes handed over a small tube which, unfurled, proved to be a sheet of hotel stationery.

Jack and I read:

> *We are being watched. The message at the desk said we had found nothing substantial and were hoping to return to Baker Street in the morning. It may put Urquhart off the scent, but I doubt it. We will learn what we can at the castle ruin. Then we shall return to Inverness with what proofs we can gather and meet you at the Inn. We have seen Urquhart. Becky and Flynn got the better of him so he will be spoiling for a fight. No word of Blinder. Preston was watching for him, but failed to turn up for a meeting with Violet last night. Becky and Flynn think this could be just as dangerous as Mycroft feared.*

"Is that last sentence a code?" Jack asked.

"It means she expects to obtain proof of the conspiracy," Holmes said. "The plot to arouse a public outcry against cholera, skew the election, and drive England from the war in South Africa."

"Can we use all this to get the Royal Navy to board Blinder's yacht?"

Holmes shook his head. "The letter is strongly suggestive to us, but not to an impartial observer. We are not in a position to offend such a valuable ally as the Americans without proof. Once we have proof, the captain of the *Daring* should be receptive."

"So, what do we do?"

"We prepare for war in Scotland," said Holmes.

Chapter 43: Becky

"At least we know Preston's still alive," Flynn said.

He had fished in his pocket for the stump of a candle, which was now lighted and secured to the floor with a pool of melted wax. The smoky, flickering light didn't even come close to reaching out to the corners of the room. But at least they could see each other, and peer into the prison cell.

"He's alive. But I'd feel a lot better about him if we knew how badly he's hurt," Becky said.

Preston hadn't moved or stirred at the sound of their voices. He was lying with his head turned out to the side, and the only sign of life Becky could see was the shallow rise and fall of his breaths.

She didn't want to call out too loudly, not when whoever had locked Preston up could be coming back to check on him. But she raised her voice just a little. "Hello? Mr. Preston, can you hear me?"

Nothing, not even a change in the pattern of his breathing.

"He could be drugged," Flynn said.

"I hope not. We're going to have an awful time carrying him out of here if he's been chloroformed."

"Carrying him?"

"Well, we can't just leave him here."

Flynn blew out a breath. "Fine. You see the key to this cell anywhere around?"

The lock on the cell's iron grating was another big, old-fashioned one.

"No. But we don't need it," Becky said. "Sneak thief's rule number two: don't waste time searching for keys when you can just pick the lock."

She pulled out the set of lock picks that Mr. Holmes had given her for Christmas.

"Just hold the light up for me?"

Flynn picked up the candle and held it near to the lock, although really what you needed even more than sight in lock-picking was your sense of touch. Luckily Mr. Holmes had given her lessons to go along with the set of picks.

Becky inserted the first of the picks, feeling inside for the lock's tumblers. It didn't take long. As well as being old, the lock was a fairly simple one. A few quick twists, and she felt it open with a metallic clang.

"Got it!" Becky pulled on the metal grill, which swung outwards.

"Well, what have we here?" The man's voice behind Becky made her jump and spin around, although not quite in time.

Urquhart.

Before she could react, Urquhart gave her a hard shove, sending her sprawling into the prison cell. Her knees connected painfully with the stone floor, but she jumped up, in time to see Urquhart pull out a gun and use it to gesture Flynn inside the cell, too.

Flynn obeyed, although at least he kept hold of the candle.

Urquhart kept the gun trained on them as he swung the metal grate shut once more. With his free hand he used a key to lock them inside.

Chapter 44: Watson

We had been sailing for about an hour, our course southeast on Loch Ness. A great long expanse of darkening water stretched out, seemingly interminably, before the prow of our vessel. Beneath the waves, I knew, the water extended downward for nearly seven hundred feet. The shoreline was about a hundred yards off to our right side, shadowy and deserted.

It was at that moment when I had my first glimpse of Urquhart Castle.

The early evening mists parted, and a ray of pale sunlight lit up a dark jagged profile on the horizon, several hundred yards away. A black, cavern-like expanse gaped forbiddingly beneath the upper rocks.

"Almost there," Jack said.

The captain was at the wheel. Gregson, Jack, Holmes and I were together in the stern.

Shortly thereafter, our vessel veered to the right.

"Distress signal over there, gentlemen," said our captain, half turning towards us.

On the shore, a man was waving a makeshift flag, probably a white shirt, with two more men on either side. Behind him a single old horse stood waiting placidly in front of a wooden dog-cart. A fourth man sat in the cart, wrapped in a blanket, shivering, his head down, clutching his shoulder.

"Do you know those men?" Holmes asked.

"No, but I can't just sail on by. In these parts we take care of each other."

"Our friend fell and broke his arm!" the man holding the flag called out. "He needs medical help in Inverness. Can we bring him on board?"

The captain called out in reply, "Yes, but I'll need to get to the castle right after." He turned to Holmes. "That way you gentlemen won't be too much delayed."

He cut the throttle, and we drifted within three feet of the shore, the nose of the boat bobbing up and down. The tide was going out, so the current brought the stern around, as if we were heading back to Inverness.

Holmes straightened. His voice was barely audible, but I caught the words plainly. "Battle stations."

He drew his pistol, holding it at his side. I did the same with my service revolver. Gregson and Jack, I knew, were unarmed.

From his position in the bow, the captain threw out a rope. The man who had spoken to us tossed his flag aside and caught the rope. Then he looped the end of the rope around a nearby tree.

"Bring your friend on board," the captain said. "Poor fella."

"Och, aye."

The words seemed to be a signal, for at that moment, the two men who had been standing with the flagman drew guns.

"Take the captain," Holmes said to Jack and Gregson. Then he shot one of the gunmen in the knee. I shot the other, in the thigh. Both were on the ground writhing, but their guns were still close at hand.

Jack and Gregson had the captain face down on the deck. "There's a pile of something here in the cabin," Jack said.

On shore, the man who had held the flag bent down to retrieve one of the guns, and Holmes shot him in the elbow.

"You, in the cart," Holmes said. "Raise your hands now."

The man looked up, glaring. I saw movement beneath the blanket. His hands were moving, but not upwards.

I shot him in the shoulder. The impact spun him around and he fell out of the cart. The pistol he had been about to fire clattered away on the roadway stones. Getting to his feet he staggered towards the woods.

Holmes shot him in the leg and he crumpled to the ground.

Then Holmes stepped over to where the captain lay prone. He placed his boot on the captain's neck.

"Watson," he said, "the tarp. Look beneath it."

In the pilot's cabin, I pulled away a thick, black canvas fabric. Around its edges sturdy metal grommets were placed at intervals, penetrating the thick hem. "Beneath the tarp are perhaps a dozen coiled ropes of medium thickness," I said.

"Toss the tarp forward to Gregson."

I did so.

Then I stood guard while Gregson and Jack spread out the tarp, dragged all four of the gunmen onto it, and forced them to stretch out, face down. Jack picked up all four guns. He handed two to Gregson and tucked one of the others into his belt. He cocked the other and pointed it at the four prone men. "Spoils of war," Jack said.

Holmes spoke to the captain. "That tarp was intended for us, was it not? You planned to make us disappear. Kill us first, I should expect."

The captain said nothing.

"Nod your head if you agree." Holmes increased the pressure

on the captain's neck. The man nodded, and I heard him croak, "Curse ye."

"You would then position our bodies on the tarp, run the ropes through the grommets, and draw up the four of us like fish in a net. You would tie a rope to the net, lash the other end to the cleat in the stern, and then drag our bodies out to the centre of the Loch. Weighted down with rocks, seven hundred feet below the surface, we should remain lost forever."

"How did you know?" the captain asked.

"The horse was calm and not a bit lathered," Holmes said. "Plainly your men were waiting, feeling no urgency to reach Inverness. An obvious ambush."

One of the men on the tarp said, "What will you do with us?" I noticed a German accent.

"The British Navy may treat you as prisoners of war," Holmes said.

"Or we may save the Navy some trouble and just make you vanish, the way you had planned to do for us," said Gregson. "After all, you're not from around here, judging from your clothes and your accent."

"No one around here would miss you, so no one would put much effort into a search for you," Jack added.

"Your captain is different, of course," Holmes said, "but probably his disappearance will be put down to a misadventure with the local monster. Still, we can keep you alive, provided you tell us exactly who you are working for."

Chapter 45: Becky

Urquhart eyed them through the iron bars, the muscles working in the side of his narrow jaw.

"Hand over the lock picks."

Becky did as she was told, tossing the lock picks through the bars to land with a clatter on the stone floor. She hadn't really expected Urquhart to be stupid enough to let her keep hold of them.

Urquhart was about to bend over to retrieve them when a blond-haired man in dark clothing entered the room, carrying a lantern.

"The ship's in and ready to be loaded, Mr. Urquhart. Is it the latest batch of crates we were supposed to bring on board?"

Urquhart swore. "No, the ones in the lower store room. Do I have to do everything myself? You." He pointed to the newcomer. "Stay here on guard while I get this sorted."

Becky held her breath.

He strode out of the room, cutting off the blond-haired man's apology in mid word.

The man gave Flynn and Becky a curious look, but then stationed himself by the door, leaning back and looking bored.

Becky released the breath that she'd been holding and darted a quick look at Flynn, who nodded.

Neither of them dared say anything or even look in that

direction, but the lock picks were still lying where Becky had tossed them on the floor outside of their prison cell.

Flynn slumped down in the cell, leaning against the metal grate so that his back was to the guard.

"Out of reach," he mouthed soundlessly.

Becky nodded. The picks lay beyond where either of them would be able to stretch an arm through the bars. And they still had the blond-haired guard to contend with before they could even think about a retrieval operation.

But she sat down next to Flynn and just as silently mouthed back, "One step closer to getting out of here is better than none."

CHAPTER 46: WATSON

"For the last time, who is paying you?"

Holmes crouched down, his tone perfectly level and reasonable.

He was eye to eye with the man who had held the white flag, who now sat before him, blood encrusting his coat sleeve from the wound in his elbow. We had bound him hand and foot, using one of the ropes that had been intended for us.

The man was watching his three partners, also bound hand and foot. The man who had been shot in the knee had passed out from the pain. The man shot in the thigh and shoulder was barely conscious. The third man, with only a thigh wound, looked downwards, avoiding his partner's gaze.

Only the captain had not been wounded. But he was securely tied up as well.

"I want a name," Holmes continued. He drew his pistol. "One of you will walk with a limp for the rest of his days. That man is unconscious and cannot respond. The others of you can. If you do not, your conditions will be worse than his. Three men. Six knees. We have more than enough bullets to ensure that none of you will ever walk or stand erect, and that every night you try to sleep will be a torment. I won't ask again."

He cocked the pistol.

"Don't know 'is name," the man finally replied. "An American.

Had a big ship in the harbour. Brought us over from Hamburg about a month ago."

"In his own ship?"

The man nodded. "He calls it *Avenger*."

"For what purpose?"

"Odd jobs."

"He pays well?"

"Better'n most."

"I shouldn't wonder," Holmes said. "He has stolen three million American dollars."

I shuddered. How many thugs and how much suffering could three million dollars unleash?

"Good for him," the man said.

"What was your last assignment?"

"Drive a carriage to London."

"The cargo?"

"Three people."

"Describe them."

"Three Scots. Two men and a woman. They said they were family, goin' to a warehouse in London for a new job. We didn't hurt 'em. Just took 'em to the warehouse. Not far from the Tower Bridge. We collected our pay and then we drove back."

"Are any other prisoners held there?"

He shook his head.

"Where, then?"

"Don't know any others," he replied. But his eyes flickered towards the south, in the direction of the castle ruin.

"Very well. Now, who told you to wait for us here today?"

The man turned towards the captain. "Him. He said it would be easy work."

Holmes stood up and walked over to stand beside the now wide-eyed captain.

Then he turned to Jack and Gregson. "I suggest the two of you perform the remainder of the interrogation."

* * *

Gregson bent down alongside the captain. Jack took the same posture on the other side. Both were in a position to whisper into each of the captain's ears. But they each spoke as Holmes had done. Quietly, in a reasonable tone.

Gregson spoke first. "Do you know why Mr. Holmes asked us to work on you?"

A moment's silence. The captain shook his head.

Then Jack. "Do you know what a dirty copper is?"

Again, the captain shook his head.

"I think you do," Gregson said.

"We need the name of the dirty copper in the Inverness Police Station," Jack said.

"We don't *like* dirty coppers," Gregson said.

"Do you want us to show you how much we don't like dirty coppers?"

"Probably he doesn't," Gregson said.

"Then he'd better give us a name. Do you understand, Captain?" Jack spoke softly, but with a menacing edge.

The captain's voice trembled. "What's to become of me?"

"If you give us a name? Same as with your German associates. It'll be up to the Navy."

"And if you don't," Gregson added, "You won't walk ever again. Only at your age, I don't think you'll be able to bear the pain."

The captain gave a name.

"We thought so," Jack said. "That's the officer we spoke to at the station. He promised to arrange everything. Now. We know you don't work for nothing. Where's the money?"

The captain gave a sigh. "Pilot's cabin."

Holmes returned from the cabin shortly thereafter with a wad of German currency, a flare gun, and a seaman's knife.

* * *

"We take the boat," Holmes said.

Gregson and Jack clambered on board. There was still steam in the boiler. Jack put more wood on the fire and turned up the throttle valve. Gregson took a position at the anchor.

Our prisoners, still tied, stared, wide-eyed and fearful. "Help us!" one of them cried.

I hesitated. It gnawed at my medical conscience not to provide any aid for their wounds, for I knew how rapidly a fatal infection could set in.

Holmes, of course, understood. "We have no time," he said.

And I, too, understood. With Lucy in danger at Urquhart Castle, to spend more time here would be unthinkable.

"So first we settle our business with Urquhart," I said.

Then I hauled myself up onto the deck.

CHAPTER 47: VIOLET

Even at the height of summer, the nights in the Scottish Highlands were unpleasantly chilly. Perched on a rocky outcropping that overlooked the Loch, Violet shivered. Although at least the wish that she had on thicker clothing was keeping her partially distracted from thinking about Preston.

She hadn't really expected to find him by simply riding a horse along the Loch road and then up to the hills surrounding to Urquhart Castle. But the fact that they'd so far not seen a sign of Preston or anyone else was like a solid lump of rock in the pit of her stomach. Well, she hadn't seen a sign of anyone. It was always possible that Lucy or Flynn and Becky were having better luck on their respective assignments.

Violet shivered again and refocused her attention on the obsidian-black waters of the Loch below her. Barely a ripple of current stirred the moonlight surface. She should have offered to search the castle ruins with Lucy instead of perching here. Flynn and Becky were bright and observant, but they were only children after all. Maybe they'd only imagined what they'd seen—

A huge dark shape loomed up out of the water, smooth and nearly silent.

Violet had to check the urge to pinch herself to make sure that she hadn't accidentally nodded off while keeping watch. Huge, with a domed body and long, serpentine neck, the monster glided through the water towards her for a breathless few moments, then vanished to the underground waterway beneath the castle.

Violet sat motionless for a few moments, the drumming of her own heartbeat loud in her ears. She'd just seen a sea monster—

No. She took herself firmly in hand. She might be cold, worried, and exhausted after going the night before without any sleep. But she still had a reasonably functional brain.

Hadn't Mr. Holmes famously said something in one of Dr. Watson's stories about eliminating the impossible?

She didn't believe in sea monsters. Therefore, the thing she'd just seen wasn't one. Therefore, someone had done an exceptionally good job of creating the appearance of a sea monster in order to frighten people away from the Loch—and maybe as a cover for some other activity here?

And Violet didn't need Sherlock Holmes's deductive abilities to formulate a theory as to who that someone might be.

The so-called monster must still be somewhere in the underground waterway, which meant that if she could get to a better vantage point, she ought to be able to get a look at the thing.

Violet stood up, brushed off her skirts, and started to pick her way slowly and carefully down the steep pitch of the slope towards the water, clutching at the small, scraggy weeds and gorse bushes that grew in the cracks between rocks. The Loch might not be infested by a monster, but she still wasn't enthusiastic about the idea of losing her balance and rolling down the slope head-first into the water.

Her palms were sweating and every tiny clatter of a pebble under her foot sounded as loud as a pistol shot. But finally, she reached a place where, by leaning out from the slope, she could just manage to peer into the narrow channel beneath the castle.

Violet drew in a quick breath.

There was a glow of light coming from lanterns strung up along the rocky walls of the channel, illumining the darkness enough that she could see what looked like a small tugboat, drawn up to a small wooden pier. And on the other side of the pier was the sea monster.

Only the dark shape was not a sea monster, she now was certain of that. It was an underwater vessel, like the drawings of submarines she had seen in books about naval history. Her grandfather's specialty had been Medieval literature, but he had enjoyed history of all kinds and one of the books in his personal library had been about the Civil War.

The vessel before Violet now reminded her of the pictures she had seen of the Confederate submarine called the *Hunley*, a large steel vessel propelled by an eight-man crew using a hand crank.

The body was long and sleek, crafted of some dark metal. The long serpentine neck still rose up to support a triangular, snake-like head. But now in the light she could see that the head and neck, too, were fashioned of metal. The lantern lights glinted on the rivets holding the contraption together.

Men were working at loading crates of what looked like glass bottles onto the underwater vessel through an open hatch in the side. Violet could hear the murmur of their voices and the chink of glass as the crates were hoisted up and brought on board.

There were words printed on the crates, but she couldn't make out the letters. Violet shifted, craning her neck as she tried to get a better look.

Silverman's—

Before she could read any more, something hard jabbed her in the ribs, and an all-too familiar voice spoke in her ear.

"Well, now. What have we here?"

Violet spun, which made her lose her balance and fall backwards, landing half-sitting and half-lying on the rocky slope.

Urquhart stood over her, a gun in his hand. Moonlight glinted in his eyes and on his teeth, which were bared in a smile.

"I thought I'd done for you, Miss Nosey."

Violet caught her breath. "Unfortunately for you, I had friends."

"Friends, is it?" Urquhart's fixed smile didn't waver. "Well, then. You'll be glad to hear that you can come with me and join three of them. Now."

He jabbed the gun in her direction, waving at her to get up.

Violet deliberated, but only briefly. If she resisted, he could easily call to the men working at loading the submarine down below them. Against Urquhart alone, she had at least a fighting chance. If he called in reinforcements, though, her odds of breaking free edged far closer to zero.

Besides, she wasn't entirely sure that she wanted to break free—at least, not yet.

She got slowly to her feet, hands raised, and said, keeping her voice light and unconcerned, "I suppose you mean that you've captured Preston, the silly idiot? But you're wrong if you think he's any friend of mine. I thought we'd been through that already."

A frown drew Urquhart's brows together. Clearly, her response hadn't been what he was expecting.

Good. Her list of potential advantages in her current situation was practically nonexistent. Especially since she'd got the better of Urquhart once before, and he wasn't likely to risk the same happening again. Even now, he was maintaining a careful distance between them, balancing on the balls of his feet and holding himself ready to move if she gave the slightest sign of being about to attack.

The best she could hope for was to keep throwing him mentally off-balance by giving him answers other than those he was expecting. She had experience with that, too, thanks to her father. Sometimes confusing him by saying something obscure or unrelated had been enough to halt him in the middle of a drunken rage, at least long enough that her mother could escape from the room.

However loud and furious her father had become, his whisky-soaked brain had retained enough of a small scrap of control that he'd never lashed out and hit Violet.

"Then I'm afraid you'll be sorry to hear that you'll have to share close quarters with Mr. Preston," Urquhart said. He smiled again. "But only very temporarily."

Violet didn't at all like the sound of that. Cold squirmed in her chest, but she kept her voice light. "Truly, a fate worse than death," she said. At the very least, she was about to find out where Preston was being held. She'd have preferred to find him without being captured, but maybe this was faster after all. "Well, lead on."

Chapter 48: Lucy

"Lead on."

I heard Violet's voice, clear and cold, ring out in the night stillness, and pressed myself further back into the shadows of a ruined stone archway.

Across an open, grassy square that had once probably been a castle courtyard, I could see Urquhart leading Violet away at gunpoint. He was trying to stay behind her, far enough that she couldn't spin around and gain control of the weapon, but his nerves were clearly on edge. He kept glancing around and quickening his pace enough that Violet could have acted if she'd wanted to, and stood a decent chance of wrestling the gun away from him.

I could guess why she hadn't acted, though, and it was for the same reason that I hadn't drawn my own Ladysmith and simply shot Urquhart in the arm or leg. I had a clear shot across the moonlit ruins, but I wasn't taking it.

I wasn't sure whether Violet had fully realised it or not. Possibly not, since her attention was likely preoccupied with Preston. But I'd heard what Urquhart had said to her, when he'd been threatening to lock her up, and he'd told her that she could join her friends. Three of them.

I wished there was another possible interpretation of those words, but I could only think of one: Becky and Flynn were prisoners, too.

Urquhart and Violet were now roughly fifty yards ahead of me, approaching the crookedly leaning tower of the ruined castle keep.

I heard Violet say, "Whose idea was it to use the legend of the Loch monster as cover for your operation here? I know it can't have been yours, it's far too clever to be something that you thought of."

I winced inwardly. Clearly, Violet had also realised that Urquhart's nerves were strained, and was working to keep him angry and distracted—enough that he would neglect to take precautions to stop her and Preston from making an attempt to escape.

But a weak, unstable criminal was often more dangerous than a strong-minded and confident one, and the danger here was that she would push Urquhart to the point of snapping. He could simply shoot Violet here. I couldn't think of too many good reasons for Urquhart to keep her alive.

"That shows what ye know," Urquhart snapped back. "This was all my idea. My idea to use the castle. My idea to hire on the useful local idiots working down below us. None of this would be possible if it hadna' been for me. The Urquhart name still means something around these parts. I put out a word here and there that I was expanding the family business to include a factory, and I had people lining up to ask for work." He barked a short laugh. "They think they're producing a new and improved health tonic."

"What about the three people you killed?" Violet asked. "The Campbell brothers and sister? I suppose they'd found out what you were actually producing and had to be got out of the way?"

Urquhart snorted. "The Campbells were too smart for

their own good. Besides, we needed bodies for the bombing. Scapegoats, in case anyone started to suspect the explosion was deliberate."

"I see. And the bonds?" Violet asked. "What's become of them?"

Urquhart laughed shortly. "I'm sure you and yer long nose would just love to know."

"Meaning that Blinder doesn't trust you enough to tell you where they are now?"

"He trusts me enough to run things here while he's away," Urquhart snapped.

To give Violet credit, she was doing an excellent job of needling him into talking.

"Away where?" Violet asked.

But Urquhart's patience had reached its limit. "That's enough questions! Stop talking and move!"

He and Violet drew further away.

I slipped out of the shadows and followed them, careful not to make any noise.

If Flynn and Becky were imprisoned somewhere in these ruins, they were also at this moment doing their level best to break free. Of that, I had absolutely no doubts. But all the same, my best chance at finding them and Preston was to follow Urquhart wherever he was taking Violet, and to hope that I could do it unseen.

I looked back over my shoulder, scanning the darkness and listening for any sounds. I'd been hoping that Jack, Holmes, and Watson would have received my message by now, and would have joined us here.

They might simply have been delayed. Or Urquhart and

Blinder—or one of their employees—might have succeeded in finding my real message, too, as well as the one I'd left at the inn's front desk.

Either way, it couldn't be helped. For the moment, with Flynn, Becky, Violet, and Preston all captured, I was on my own.

Chapter 49: Becky

The sound of footsteps made Becky freeze, her heart skittering against her ribcage.

The big stone blocks that made up the floor of their cell were cold and uncomfortable to sit on, but at least Flynn had put the stump of their candle in the middle of the cell so that they had light enough to see.

Their guard had a lantern, too, but he was still all the way over by the door, and the light only just barely reached them. Most of the big underground room was covered with patches of dark shadow.

Becky had been in the act of trying to slowly and silently work the lace on one of her boots free. For the moment, she couldn't think of a way of getting the lock picks back without their guard seeing. But still going on the theory that any step towards escape was better than none, she wanted to be prepared to at least try to snag them through the prison bars if they got the chance.

Now she dropped her hands and tucked both her feet under her, praying that she wouldn't be forced to stand up.

Preston was still unconscious, and they hadn't wanted to risk drawing the guard's notice by trying to wake him. He still hadn't moved, groaned, or even flickered an eyelid, so Becky was fairly sure that they weren't going to be able to count on him for any help.

Flynn had been keeping a covert eye on their guard, ready to nudge her if he showed any signs of leaving his post. Now at the sound of someone coming, Flynn slumped further down against the iron cell bars and gave a quiet snore, doing a convincing impression of being sound asleep.

Becky didn't want to call attention to herself by turning around, but as the footsteps entered their underground room, she heard the guard say, "Mr. Urquhart."

Her stomach dropped. That was exactly who she'd been hoping the new arrival wouldn't be.

Urquhart's voice growled, "Another one for you to watch. Caught her sneaking around along the edge of the waterway."

Becky's heart went from racing to lying dead in her chest. She darted a quick look over her shoulder, and a wave of relief washed through her when she saw that the woman Urquhart was pushing was Violet, not Lucy. The relief made her feel a bit guilty, but she couldn't help being overwhelmingly thankful that Lucy hadn't been captured.

Violet was pale, but she didn't look as though she'd been hurt. She didn't say anything, and her attention was fixed on the cell. Becky guessed that she was staring past them to where Preston was still lying sprawled on the floor.

"Yes, sir." The blond-haired guard nodded as Urquhart shoved Violet towards the cell door. He cleared his throat, sounding awkward. "I understand we can't have any strangers or competitors snooping around. But them?"

Out of the corner of her eye, Becky saw him gesture towards her and Flynn, still looking nervous, but awkwardly determined to say what he was thinking.

"I mean to say, they're just a couple of children."

Urquhart paused in the middle of giving Violet another shove towards the cell. He had a gun in one hand, and Becky could practically see the thought cross his mind that maybe he should just shoot the blond-haired man here and now before he asked too many more inconvenient questions.

But he must have decided against it, because after a second or two, Urquhart turned, his mouth stretched in the least convincing smile that Becky had ever seen.

"We'll make sure that they get back to their parents after we finish our operations tonight. Mr. Blinder and I just don't want them getting in the way or causing any trouble." He gave a laugh that was even more unconvincing than his smile. "You know what children can be."

The blond-haired man still looked doubtful. Becky wondered whether it would do any good if she spoke up. Maybe she could convince him to ignore Urquhart's orders and help them. But probably that would just make Urquhart more likely to start shooting.

"Yes, sir," the guard finally answered.

"Good. And I'll make sure that you're paid a bonus for tonight's work," Urquhart told him.

Becky didn't believe for a second that a bonus was actually what the blond-haired man was going to get tonight. Unless you counted a coffin as a bonus.

But he looked a bit happier as he nodded at Urquhart. "Thank you, sir."

Just like Flynn had pointed out, people who were paid enough usually did decide to stop asking questions.

"Watch them while I finish things outside," Urquhart told the guard. He unlocked the cell door.

Violet was being very quiet, and she didn't even try to fight back or resist as Urquhart pushed her inside, and then slammed the door closed again. Becky took that to mean that she must have some sort of plan. She looked at Flynn and Becky and gave a slight shake of her head, as though she was warning them not to try anything, either.

She needn't have worried. Becky was holding her breath, waiting to see whether Urquhart would notice that one of her boot laces was halfway undone, or remember the lock picks that were still lying on the floor outside of their cell. They were lucky that the room was so dark and shadowy. Becky knew exactly where the picks had landed, and even she could only just barely make out their faint metallic gleam in the flickering lantern light.

Urquhart locked their door and pocketed the key.

"I'll be back in under an hour," he told the guard.

Becky's heart constricted. Under an hour didn't give them much time. And she still didn't have any idea how they were going to stop the guard from seeing them, even if she did finish freeing her boot lace and worked out a way to use it to retrieve the lock picks.

Urquhart strode out. The guard remained where he was by the door, although Becky saw that he kept giving them quick glances that were half nervous, half puzzled.

He was probably starting to realise that this whole operation wasn't actually about producing health tonics.

Violet didn't look at either Flynn or Becky again, but she said under her breath, "How good are you at screaming and pretending to cry?"

Flynn stared, but Becky immediately answered, "Very."

"Good," Violet whispered. "In that case, I'm having an epileptic seizure."

Becky didn't even have time to react or answer. Without saying another word, Violet keeled over onto the floor, writhing and thrashing and making awful groaning, choking noises.

Becky screamed. "Help! She's having a fit—a seizure! Help—oh, please, help." She stood at the door of the cell and called out to the guard. "Please, she needs a doctor, or she'll die!"

Becky had thought she was fairly good at theatricals, after all of Lucy's coaching. But her performance was nothing to Violet's. If Becky hadn't known better, she would have honestly thought that Violet was dying. Her head flopped helplessly on her neck, her eyes rolled up, and she kept making the terrible gurgling sounds.

The guard, wide-eyed with alarm, picked up his lantern and sped towards them across the room, reaching the door of the cell and peering down at them through the bars.

In a movement so quick that Becky would have sworn her body actually blurred, Violet sprang up, seized hold of the guard's upper arms through the gaps between their prison bars and yanked him forward, crashing his head into the metal door frame.

He didn't even cry out, just slid to the ground, unconscious.

Becky and Flynn stared.

Violet turned and without missing a beat said, briskly, "I have a pistol, too." She drew a gun that looked similar to Lucy's from an inner pocket of her coat. "I did my best to make sure that Urquhart would be too distracted to search me for weapons—which he was. But I didn't want to shoot our guard here." She nodded to the unconscious man on the ground. "For one, he probably doesn't deserve it, and for another, the noise of the shot might have brought reinforcements. It looks as though we might have to risk it now, though." She was eyeing the barred metal door of their cell. "I can't think of any other way out of here than to shoot the lock off."

"Not a good idea. Close space like this with stone walls? There's a solid chance that the bullet will go ricocheting around and hurt—possibly kill—someone."

The voice came from the back of the cell. Spinning around, Becky saw Preston sitting up and looking at all of them.

Violet startled, then her expression turned one of the strangest blends of relief and annoyance that Becky had ever seen.

"How long have you been playing possum?"

"Long enough." Preston had a trickle of blood on the side of his face and a bruise on his jaw, but he got to his feet only a little unsteadily.

All the other times that Becky had seen him, his expression had looked so calm that he seemed almost on the verge of falling asleep. But now his face creased in a scowl as he faced Violet.

"I was hoping you'd be smart enough to avoid winding up here."

"Me?" Violet glared back at him. "What about you? If only there had been some way of avoiding your current predicament. Something that involved, oh, I don't know, telling someone what your plans were instead of going off on your own and winding up getting captured and locked in an underground dungeon?"

"As opposed to your standard method of operations," Preston growled back.

"Yes!" Violet faced him, bright spots of colour appearing in her cheeks. "And it's not been working out particularly well for me. How has it been working for you?"

"If they keep going like this, Urquhart's not even going to have to bother getting rid of them," Flynn said to Becky under his breath. "They'll kill each other before he even gets back."

"Lock picks," Becky said. "They're still our best chance of getting out of this cell. And here." She bent over, tugging her boot lace the rest of the way free. "We can use this, maybe. Do you have anything we could use to make a hook?"

Violet and Preston were still arguing, making references that Becky didn't understand, but that she assumed were about cases from back in America.

Flynn rummaged through his pockets, coming up with two pencil stubs, a book of safety matches, and the broken stem of a pipe before holding out a small twist of wire that looked like it had probably once held the cork of a glass bottle in place. "How's this?"

"Perfect."

Becky bent the wire into a curved hook shape, then tied it to the end of the lace. She threaded her arm through the bars, then tossed the hook out towards the ring holding the lock picks together.

The wire landed on top of the picks, but didn't hook them.

Flynn blew out a breath.

Becky pulled the lace back and looked over, searching the darkness at the entrance to the room. Urquhart had said he'd be back in under an hour, but what exactly did that mean? He could step through the doorway any second, or they might have thirty minutes or more.

Either way, though, time was ticking by alarmingly.

Becky tried again. This time, the wire hooked the lock pick's metal ring, but slid off again when she tugged at the lace.

Flynn shifted his weight restlessly. "Shooting would be faster. Maybe we should ask Violet for her gun, if we can stop her and Preston going at it hammer and tongs for long enough."

"No." Becky shook her head. "Preston is right. It might be

faster, but if the bullet does bounce off a wall and hit you, you'll be a lot deader, too."

She tossed the wire and boot lace out again, and this time, succeeded in hooking the lock picks and dragging them several inches across the stones.

Flynn stretched out on the floor, reaching an arm through the cell bars.

"Got 'em!" He snagged the lock picks, pulled them in, and handed them over to Becky. "Can you manage from this side?"

"I think so."

It was harder, working from inside the cell. But after a few moments of fumbling, Becky felt the lock tumblers lift, slide, and then snap open with a click.

Preston and Violet were still fighting, although Preston seemed to be getting the worst of it, because he'd resorted to a low, wordless growl of frustration.

"Oh, now there's a brilliant argument," Violet snapped. "That would be so intimidating if we were in the middle of a forest and you were a grizzly bear. But unfortunately for you, we're not and you're not."

Flynn put his thumb and forefinger between his teeth and whistled softly.

Both Preston and Violet jumped and spun to stare at him.

"Becky's got the cell door open," Flynn said. He gave the iron bars a shove so that they swung outwards. "Can we get out of here now?"

He'd actually succeeded in silencing them both. They stared at him for a full half second before nodding.

Becky put the lock picks back in her pocket and followed Flynn out of the cell, with Preston and Violet coming close behind—

Just as Urquhart stepped through the door to the underground room.

Urquhart looked shocked for a beat, then drew his gun, aiming it at them.

Panic tore through Becky's chest. Violet would still have her own pistol, but she didn't have it ready. And in the time it took her to pull the pistol out and aim, Urquhart could shoot at least one of them.

The silence seemed to stretch on for ages, although really it was probably only a second or two.

Then Preston kicked over the lantern on the floor, plunging the room into darkness.

"Run!"

Becky didn't need to be told twice. Urquhart yelled something, and then a gunshot rang out, the sound loud enough to feel like a hammer strike against her eardrums. But she didn't feel anything, so the bullet couldn't have hit her.

She grabbed hold of Flynn's hand and sprinted for where she judged the door to be.

CHAPTER 50: VIOLET

"Should we be worried about the children?" Violet gasped.

She and Preston were pounding down some sort of corridor. The tunnel itself was unlighted, but there was a faint electric glow coming from up ahead, allowing her to see, and there was no sign of either Becky or Flynn.

She'd lost track of them after Preston had knocked over the lamp and ordered everyone to run. She'd assumed that they had gotten around Urquhart and out of the room ahead of them, but now doubt pinched her. Maybe Urquhart had grabbed them after all.

"I'd say they've done pretty well for themselves so far," Preston answered back.

That was embarrassingly true. While she and Preston had been trading insults, Flynn and Becky had calmly unlocked the door of their cell.

Proof, as though she'd needed any more, of just what a terrible idea any further association with Preston would be.

"Where are we?" she asked.

"Sorry, fresh out of maps to this place." Preston sounded almost back to his ordinary self. "I was just figuring that whatever we find up ahead was better than where we were be—"

He cut off speaking abruptly.

They had almost reached the glowing square of electric light, which Violet could now see was a doorway into a larger, lighted chamber. She caught just a glimpse of some complicated-looking apparatus inside: pipes and tubes surrounding an enormous central vat. But for the most part her view was blocked by the two men who had just stepped through the doorway.

Two armed men. Both carried rifles slung over their shoulders.

Violet froze, her heart trying to leap up into her throat. "I think I've spotted a flaw in your reasoning," she told Preston under her breath.

She wasn't looking directly at him, but even out of the corner of her eye, she could tell that he was evaluating their options and the likelihood that they would die if they tried to fight. Or they could turn and run, but the most probable outcome there was getting shot in the back.

That left only one option that Violet could see, however much she didn't like it: surrender.

Preston must have come to the same conclusion, because he slowly raised his hands. Violet raised hers, as well.

The electric lights behind the armed men went out, plunging them into instant, inky blackness so suddenly that it was like a slap across the face.

"What did you—" Violet started to ask.

"Wasn't me this time," Preston said. "Come on."

Up ahead, Violet could hear the armed men stumbling and cursing in the dark. But from behind came the sound of running footsteps. Urquhart?

Preston seemed to think so, because he grabbed hold of her hand and raced forward. Ordinarily, Violet would have wrenched away and informed him that she was perfectly capable of running on her own. But she had to admit that there was some sense in staying together and not tripping or blundering into one another in the pitch black.

Preston was a few steps ahead of her, and she heard a thud as he must have collided with one of the armed guards. The man's breath went out in an audible *oof*, and Violet heard the second thud of him landing on the stone floor.

Preston kept running, then slowed as the sounds around them changed. Instead of the close, echoing confines of the tunnel, Violet felt a wider open space around them. At least a dozen voices, some frightened, others angry, were calling out, demanding to know what had happened and why the electric generator had suddenly failed.

Violet's heart seized up as she recognised one of the voices: Flynn—she was sure it was the boy Flynn—saying, as though through gritted teeth, "Let go of me!"

The lights flashed on again, the sudden brightness equally shocking after the darkness of the past few minutes.

Violet's first sight after her vision cleared was of Becky and Flynn, both of them struggling in the grip of more armed men with rifles.

She and Preston were bound to be next. The room was crowded with workers in white coveralls, which made the two of them in their ordinary clothes stand out like a couple of sore thumbs.

The second that the guards noticed them—and they would—they'd be held at gunpoint and marched straight back to the prison cell.

But even as that thought flashed through Violet's mind, a clear voice rang out, cutting across the excited talking all around.

"Stop!"

Violet's head jerked up to see Lucy.

Lucy had climbed up to the top of a high metal platform, directly above the room's central vat. With one hand, she was gripping a chain that seemed to control the flow of liquid to a row of spigots. Her eyes were fixed on a point somewhere behind Violet, and, turning, Violet saw Urquhart standing in the doorway.

Lucy spoke again, her voice calm and yet granite hard.

"Order your men to let Flynn and Becky go," she said. "Otherwise, I'm going to pull this chain and expose everyone in the room to the poison you're brewing here."

Chapter 51: Watson

In the gathering shadows, we sailed our vessel along the coast for nearly a half hour.

Then, at the tiller, Holmes said, "Cut power."

Up ahead, we saw the massive jagged stone towers of Urquhart Castle, perhaps a hundred yards away. They loomed high above us, dark, silent, and foreboding.

Gregson closed the steam valves and Jack disengaged the drive shaft.

We drifted, silent, towards the yawning cavern at the base of the castle. Faint moonlight on the water revealed a water channel and another boat very like ours, alongside a wooden dock. On the other side of the dock lay something large, metallic, and glistening.

The dock itself appeared deserted. But the boat and the metallic object, likely a steel-clad vessel, blocked access.

Then I saw a rowboat, at anchor not far away.

Holmes, at the tiller, saw it too, and steered alongside.

"Drop anchor," he said.

I did so. Gregson and Jack used a barge-pole to pull the rowboat over to the side of our vessel.

"Stoke up the fire and choke down the vents," Holmes said. "We may need to get up steam quickly upon our return."

That task accomplished, we boarded the rowboat, one by

one. Gregson took the oars. Silently he propelled us past the two vessels and the dock, and into the narrow water channel that led into a cavern beneath the castle.

Small lamps on the walls of the channel cast a spectral glow.

The water grew more and more shallow. I could see that we would run aground in only a few yards.

Then the lights went out, and we were plunged into darkness.

We waited. Seconds later, the lights came on again, and we heard a woman's voice call out, sharp and commanding: "Stop!"

"That's Lucy!" Jack said. "By God—"

Drawing both pistols, he dashed forward as though propelled by a gunpowder charge.

We followed.

CHAPTER 52: LUCY

"Poison?"

Several gasps and a murmur of frightened voices ran around the room.

"Poison?"

"What is she talking about?"

"What does she mean?"

"She's lying!" Urquhart's shout cut across the uproar. "We're manufacturing a health tonic, nothing more. I warned you about looking out for agents of our competitors trying to sabotage us. She's one of them!"

I was trying not to let myself look at Flynn and Becky. Right now, I couldn't afford any distractions. But I could see them, held fast by two armed guards. Neither was struggling for the moment. I just had to hope that they stayed still and silent. This would all be immeasurably harder if they did anything to get themselves hauled deeper into the castle's underground complex.

I addressed the crowd. "I'm not here for sabotage, I'm not working for anyone but myself—and all of you. I'm here to help—"

Urquhart cut me off, spinning to one of the armed guards. "Shoot her!"

The room fell silent, the crowd of workers hushed.

The guard didn't move, only looked from Urquhart to me and back again, his expression doubtful.

The flaw in Urquhart's claim was that the men hired to safeguard the ingredients of a health tonic, however secret, weren't generally expected to commit murder to protect the operation.

"Mr. Urquhart is the one who's lying." I took advantage of the momentary hush to raise my voice again.

My muscles were tense with the awareness that my position was flawed, too, by the fact that my threat to unleash the poison was nothing but a bluff. There was no possible way that I could expose at least forty innocent workers to poison. The best I could hope for was to turn the tide of their opinion against Urquhart.

"If the liquid in this vat really is nothing more than a health tonic," I called out to Urquhart, "Then that should be easy enough to prove. Why don't you come over here and drink some of it?"

Urquhart's jaw worked. "It's ... it's not ready yet. Drinking the tonic before it's fully developed could have side effects—"

Another murmur of doubt ran through the crowd, uncertain whispers and angry mutters. Urquhart was about to lose all control of them, and he knew it.

His face twisted. "Curse it, I'll attend to her myself!"

He scrambled up the scaffolding, swinging himself up onto the platform, his pistol raised.

Chapter 53: Lucy

I held myself very still, wondering whether I could risk attacking Urquhart. The other weakness in my position was that I was currently exposed on all sides, as much of an easy target as though I had painted bright red concentric circles on my forehead.

If the guards were loyal to Urquhart, they could shoot me in an instant. But on the other hand, Urquhart almost certainly would shoot me if I let him.

Before I could make up my mind, a shot rang out, not from Urquhart's gun but from down below.

The pistol flew out of Urquhart's grasp. He gave a yell of pain, clutching his hand.

Looking down, I saw Holmes, Watson, Gregson, and Jack were pushing their way through the crowd.

Watson and Gregson were disarming the guards. Jack was the one who had fired at Urquhart; the revolver was still in his raised hand.

Urquhart gave another yell, this time of pure rage, and rushed at me.

I let him come within a step or two, then seized hold of his wrist and twisted, dragging him forward.

Urquhart stumbled, staggered past me, and then lost his balance, teetering on the edge of the platform.

For an endless moment, he seemed to hover there, his arms

flailing, his face contorted in panic. Then he toppled backwards, landing with a splash in the vat below.

"Stay back!" Holmes barked.

One or two of the guards had made a move to help Urquhart, and even Watson had taken an uncertain step or two in the direction of the vat.

All of them froze, though, at the sound of Holmes's voice.

"If you value your lives, do not come one step closer to that liquid," Holmes commanded in the same ringing tone. "If you touch it, you will suffer an agonizing death within a matter of days."

I could see Urquhart below, splashing, choking and struggling inside the vat. The walls were perhaps four feet high.

The entire room watched as though frozen as he managed to haul himself up to the top edge of the vat and clamber over, clothes dripping, the hair plastered to his forehead.

He had drawn a knife and now clutched the hilt, his teeth bared as he started to charge towards Holmes.

Another shot rang out, this time from Watson's service revolver.

Urquhart clutched his chest, toppled over, and this time lay still.

Chapter 54: Lucy

"A very fine shot, Sergeant Kelly," I said, less than a minute later. "Catching Urquhart's wrist and knocking away his gun."

"I was aiming for his heart," Jack said.

"Oh, well. Pistols are just so unreliable these days, aren't they?" I said.

And kissed him.

CHAPTER 55: WATSON

"Outside, everyone," Holmes said. "To the boats. Fire up the boilers and wait for me."

On our way, we all passed by the body that had once been Urquhart. It lay sprawled on the stone floor of the cave, eyes wide, sightless, dully lit by the electric light.

"Horrible," said one of the workers.

"A horrible man," said another. "And horrible to think that we trusted him."

"We might at the least shut his eyes," said a third. "He is a human being, after all."

"He is highly toxic," I said. "Do not touch him. Stay well back, as you value your lives."

* * *

Outside, the moonlight shimmered on the dark waters of the Loch. We waited for more orders from Holmes.

The employees and guards had filled the second boat, the one on which they had come. Their boiler was lit, and smoke issued from the stack. On our boat, the one that had brought us to the castle, Flynn, Becky, Lucy, Preston, Violet, and I watched Jack and Gregson as they fired up our boiler. We had lashed the submarine boat to the stern of our vessel, after first sealing its watertight doors. The rowboat that Flynn and Becky had 'borrowed' floated near the dock, at the end of its tether rope.

We waited for Holmes.

I knew we had a long night ahead of us. First, the treacherous captain of our vessel and his four would-be henchmen, now our wounded prisoners, would have to be rescued and brought along. Then we needed to travel seventeen miles to the River Ness channel lock, and then another mile north beyond it to the Inverness Harbour, to reach the Royal Navy destroyer *Daring*. Since the Inverness police had betrayed us, the Royal Navy was our only hope of enforcing justice.

We waited.

The glow from the string of electrical lights shone pale yellow inside the passage to the cavern. The silence was broken only by the night breeze, the rustle of the waves on the rocky shore, and the steady, deep, thrumming of the electrical generator coming from inside the cave.

Then, on the dock, an eerie lean figure appeared, silhouetted against the electric glow from the passageway. It was Holmes. He held something in his hand.

"Cast off," he called. "Get well away!"

We did so.

Holmes walked back inside the cave and we could see him no longer.

There came the crack of a pistol shot, and the whoosh of a flare gun. Then, three events, nearly simultaneous: a great loud thunderclap of an explosion, massive and reverberating, a flash of light from within the cave, and a roar of falling rocks. Our boat swayed as the explosion shook the ground beneath the cave. The electric lights went out, and our boat rocked on more waves. I struggled to see into the cave, looking for Holmes. I saw only blackness. Then my eyes adjusted. The moonlight, faint as it was, illuminated a figure moving on the dock.

It was Holmes, running. At the end of the dock, he did not pause for even a split second as he made a graceful dive, his lean body flattening out, straight as a javelin as he hit the water.

The sound of his splash was nearly obscured by the grinding roar of rocks as the cave collapsed entirely. A cloud of dust arose. When it cleared, the dock was no longer visible. I saw only a sloping wall of dark rubble. The cave entrance and everything within had been sealed off by the landslide.

Holmes swam to the rowboat and scrambled in. A moment later he was at the oars, heading towards us.

**

Our plan very nearly worked.

We were alongside HMS *Daring* by mid-morning. The harbour tender that had taken us to Urquhart Castle had brought us through the River Ness lock. From there we took a water taxi, leaving the tender boat and its captain behind, guarded by Jack. The wounded prisoners were on shore in the dog-cart, guarded by Gregson.

Marcus Dover, the captain of the *Daring,* remembered Holmes, and, of course, gave permission for us all to come on board. He said he had orders to render us every assistance the regulations would allow, courtesy of Mycroft Holmes and Commissioner Edward Bradford. A crisp, compact leader with a seaman's rolling gait, he listened attentively as Holmes described the events of the previous night. Lucy, Preston, Flynn and Becky added details from time to time.

When our narrative concluded, Captain Dover quickly dispatched a launch to pick up the wounded prisoners from the dog-cart and bring them, with Gregson, to the sick bay of the *Daring*.

Then Holmes outlined his method to prove that Blinder, the American criminal, was behind the plan to endanger the lives of thousands of Londoners with the deadly ricin poison. Captain Dover agreed that with such proof, he would have full power to order the boarding and search of the *Avenger* and the arrest of those involved.

We then put the plan into operation.

A Navy launch took Holmes and me close to the shore, where we boarded the harbour tender. A young Navy lieutenant named Williams was with us, intending to witness the proceedings from close range.

The traitorous captain was still on board the harbour tender, guarded by Jack Kelly. The man was eager to cooperate in exchange for what he hoped would be lenient treatment.

We set out for the *Avenger*. Tied astern of our boat, the submarine trailed behind at a few yards' distance. Harsh daylight revealed the mechanical nature of its black metal top and neck-like tower.

In the meantime, the *Daring* had manoeuvred closer.

We approached Blinder's yacht, an imposing steel-clad vessel, perhaps a hundred feet long. We crouched behind the pilot's cabin of our vessel, against some boxes that hid us from the American craft.

At a nod from Holmes, the captain called out, "Ahoy, *Avenger*! Stand by to take cargo!"

A harsh voice came from the *Avenger*, calling down in reply: "Why are you late?"

Holmes and I each risked a look. I had a glimpse of a green-uniformed man, dark-bearded and wearing a captain's cap, looking down from the bridge of the *Avenger*.

"Submarine's drive train broke," our captain said. "Ruddy nuisance."

"Stand by."

There came a rattle of chains from above, and then we saw a lifeboat swing away from the hull of the *Avenger*, being lowered by a winch somewhere up on deck.

A moment later we saw two burly sailors, also in green uniforms, in the lifeboat. As the lifeboat hit the water with a loud slap, one of the two sailors said, "Open the hatch."

"You do it," our captain said. "I don't want to get near that stuff."

"Old milksop," said the other sailor. He used one of the oars to hook the towing rope, bringing the submarine closer.

Then he clambered easily onto the top, unsnapping the clamps, and lifting the hatch. He knelt down for a long moment. Then he turned to his companion. "Smells all right. Nothing looks broken."

Holmes and the young Navy lieutenant exchanged nods.

The lieutenant pulled a flare gun from his coat and fired it into the air. The flare burst into red streamers, making a loud pop. A moment later we heard a loud foghorn blast from the *Daring*.

Holmes, Jack, and I stepped out into the open, guns drawn and cocked.

"Raise your hands," Holmes said.

"You are under arrest and in the custody of Her Majesty's Navy," said the young lieutenant. "If you move, you will be shot dead."

***

As I said, the plan very nearly worked.

A short while later, all of us were on board the *Daring,* along with one Harry Romain, the American captain of the *Avenger*. Young Lieutenant Williams had seen enough to prove complicity in the poisoning scheme.

However, Romain denied any knowledge that the crates and bottles carried by the submarine had contained poison. They were merely herbal tonics, he insisted, intended for legitimate sale in London.

Also, he insisted, the owner of the *Avenger* was not on board. "Mr. Blinder remained in Amsterdam. He had some business to attend to. Now, I demand that you release me and allow me to return to Amsterdam to fulfil my obligations to my employer."

Captain Dover said, "We will search your ship and hold you in custody until the search is complete."

He dispatched a Navy search party, headed by Lieutenant Williams.

We waited. Captain Dover had refreshments brought.

None of us had an appetite, save for Flynn and Becky.

It seemed an eternity, but, in reality, could not have been more than an hour. Then Lieutenant Williams returned, solemn-faced.

"We found nothing," the young lieutenant said.

The American captain stood up and spread his arms wide in a theatrical gesture. "What did I tell you?" He grinned, triumphant. "Now you must release me."

My heart sank.

But then I heard Flynn's voice. "'Ere now! 'E's one of the kidnappers!"

Flynn came forward, pointing his finger at the American captain. "You're the one who drove the coach in London! You hauled out Miss Violet in that wicker hamper! I saw you!"

"I deny it." Romain's face was a frozen mask.

"Mr. Flynn is, in my experience, a most reliable witness." said Holmes.

"To repeat, I deny it," said the American. "Now, release me."

"I suggest that prior to any release of this man, further investigation is warranted," Holmes said.

"Agreed," said Captain Dover.

Holmes gestured towards Violet Leverton. "Further, I request Miss Leverton here be allowed to conduct a further inspection of the *Avenger*. She has personal knowledge of the history and background of its American owner."

"Permission granted," said Captain Dover.

The American captain's expression had changed from triumph to disbelief, and then to rage. "I demand to see the American Ambassador!" he shouted.

He stood, arms folded, defiant, now speaking with a more sinister, threatening tone. "You all will pay for this outrage. You can count on that. You have been warned. You will be defeated."

I felt a foreboding, a hollow emptiness that somehow gave credence to the American's threats. Three million dollars in bearer bonds, I thought. So much evil could be accomplished with all that money. More police could be corrupted. More suffering and havoc could be unleashed. So many more battles might be fought. So many more, and there could be no certainty of victory. And every day the odds increased that our own defeat might come.

I saw a shadow move on the dark waters alongside the *Daring*. The harbour surface had been utterly still in the moonlight, but now, suddenly, there was movement, perhaps ten yards away from the ship's side. As though something huge swam, unseen, beneath the surface. I felt a shiver run the length of my spine.

The submarine?

No, Captain Dover's men had taken possession of that devilish mechanism more than an hour ago.

What, then? Was this another submarine? Or had the monster of rumour and legend now somehow come to life?

For a long moment I stared into the dark waters.

Then, I looked upwards. I saw a passing cloud, covering the moon.

And Captain Dover broke the silence, addressing two of his men and gesturing towards the American captain. "Put him in the brig. He is to be held pending results of further investigation."

Dover's men propelled the American away.

Still feeling vaguely unsettled, I turned to Holmes. "Holmes, you don't suppose—"

He gave one of his fleeting little smiles. "As I have observed before, Watson, this agency stands flat-footed upon the ground," he said. "No sea monsters need trouble us. Our fellow humans can create horrors enough."

CHAPTER 56: VIOLET

Violet swung herself over the metal railing that ran around the prow of Blinder's yacht, dropping lightly down onto the deck. For all she knew, the seamen of the British Navy who had searched the *Avenger* could have been right. Blinder's private vessel might very well be empty of both Blinder and any trace of the bonds.

It wasn't that Violet didn't believe that they'd made an effort to search thoroughly, so much as that she wanted to confirm for herself that the yacht was clear.

Cases didn't always wrap up with a nice neat bow: justice served, stolen goods returned, and the criminal locked up safely behind bars. Violet had learned that within her first week at Pinkerton's.

But if she had to go back to America without any idea of what had ultimately become of the stolen bonds and with Blinder still a free man, she was going to have an even nastier taste in her mouth than she usually got from an unfinished case.

She straightened, surveying the deck with its gleaming polished boards and white deck chairs arranged in a row along one side. The chairs were all stamped in gold with a stylised A for *Avenger*. A shuffleboard court had been marked out in the open space nearest the ship's prow.

"How the other half lives, right?" Preston's voice drawled behind her.

Violet managed not to jump. She should have been expecting that Preston would find his way here, too, with or without Captain Dover's permission.

She turned around just as he was swinging himself over the side railing to join her.

"I take it that you don't believe our friend the captain's solemn assurance that Blinder and the bonds have disappeared, either?" she asked.

"Call it a hunch." Preston raised an eyebrow at her. The bruises from tonight's misadventures still stood out livid on his face, but his voice was calm. "What, no arguments against my joining your search efforts? Are you starting to appreciate my sterling worth?"

"Maybe I'm just tired of fighting with you."

Violet turned away before she could say anything else—or before her expression could give away the relief she'd felt at the sight of Preston.

A small part of her actually felt safer with him here. And what did that mean?

"Where do you think we should start?" Preston asked.

"I'm not sure." Violet took another slow survey of their surroundings. A doorway straight ahead led to what she assumed were the cabins. "If you were a narcissistic criminal with a practically unlimited supply of money, where would you hide something?"

Preston frowned, considering. "It'd have to be somewhere none of the ship's crew were likely to find it. Though that doesn't help much. A ship this size, you could tuck away about a thousand bond certificates and no one would know the difference."

"One thing," Violet said. "I don't think it's actually the bonds that we're looking for anymore."

Both Preston's eyebrows went up this time, but he said, "You think they've already been cashed in?"

"That would be my guess. Urquhart slipped just a bit last night, when he was holding me at gunpoint. He said that Blinder had left him in charge of their operations at the castle while he—Blinder—travelled somewhere. I'll admit I can't prove it, but my guess would be that he sailed this yacht to Germany and cashed in the bonds for German marks."

Preston considered, then nodded slowly. "Makes sense. We already knew or suspected that there was German money behind all of this, and Blinder could have taken this boat to a port city like Hamburg, then sailed back here. That's good thinking."

"Thank you." Violet ignored the warm glow she felt at the compliment. This was getting entirely out of hand. She led the way to the cabin door. "We may as well start in Blinder's private quarters. He won't have hidden the money anywhere obvious like under the bed. But at the same time, I'd imagine that he'd want to keep his fortune close by."

The *Avenger*'s cabins were just as luxurious as the rest of the ship. Silk coverlets graced the beds, and gold water taps adorned the wash rooms. The furniture was all designed in the French style, as though Louis XIV had tried to cram the palace of Versailles into a yacht's state rooms.

Preston's lip curled in faint distaste as they entered the largest of the cabins, which Violet assumed was Blinder's. He opened up one of the drawers in the big mahogany wardrobe, revealing a stack of silk pyjamas and dressing gowns.

His lip curled further as he sorted rapidly through the silken heap.

"Likes his creature comforts, doesn't he?" Then Preston looked up at her. "What are your plans after this? Would you take back your old job at Pinkerton's, if it was offered?"

Violet was surprised, both by the question and by the fact that Preston had bothered to ask it.

"No one's offered me my old job back."

"Mr. Pinkerton would, if you turn up with the stolen money, ready to hand it all back to the US Treasury Department."

That was true enough, and it had been what Violet was counting on, all this time: Mr. Pinkerton would love nothing more than to claim that the millions of stolen dollars had been recovered by one of his agents.

"So you're finally admitting that I stand a better chance of finding the money than you?"

Preston grinned briefly, but then sobered. "It never sat right with me, your getting kicked off the Pinkerton's staff," he said. "I wanted you to know that."

This night really did keep getting progressively stranger. Violet shrugged. "Thank you. But it's all over and done with now."

Thankfully Preston allowed the change of subject to stand. "It won't be enough to just find the German marks," he said.

"True." Violet moved towards the big four-poster bed that sat in the middle of the room, atop a plush oriental rug. She should be focused on the search. She knew that. But at the same time, she couldn't stop herself from darting a quick look at Preston.

For her entire career as a detective, both at Pinkerton's and as a lone agent, she had worked alone. Always. She tracked down leads, she evaluated evidence, found patterns, built her case, and came to a conclusion without anyone else's voice in her mind but her own.

This—working alongside someone, talking over not only the case but also her own personal plans—was entirely new territory.

"We have to hope that Blinder will have kept a record from the sale of the bonds," she said out loud. "Otherwise even a pile of German marks is just that—a pile of foreign currency. Nothing to show that it should be returned the Treasury."

Preston started to pull open another drawer, but then stopped, straightening. "Anything strike you about this room?" he asked.

He was frowning, his gaze travelling around the four walls.

"I assume you don't mean Mr. Blinder's appalling taste in furniture and clothing," Violet said. Now that Preston mentioned it, she knew—or thought she knew—what he meant. The proportions of the room seemed just a bit off, based on what they'd already seen of the cabin next door.

The walls were all made of gleaming mahogany panelling, and the one behind the bed should have been pushed back by at least a couple of feet. Not to mention that it was odd, having the bed squarely in the centre of the room rather than standing with the headboard against the back wall, the way most people would have arranged—

One of the panels in the back wall flew open and Blinder, wild-eyed and sweating, burst out of the hiding space.

Before Violet could react or even fully process what had happened, Blinder had seized hold of her, twisting her so that her back was pressed up against his front, and jabbed the barrel of a gun into her temple.

"Don't come any closer," he told Preston. "Unless you want her brains spattered on the walls."

Preston was holding very still, his muscles taut, as though his whole body was knitted together with coiled tension. His eyes were half-lidded with the lazy look that Violet knew hid furious thinking, but he drawled, "They're your walls, friend. But you do realise that even if you shoot her, there's no way you're getting out of here."

Probably Blinder did realise that, but he was long past the point of being able to see reason. The hand holding the gun shook, so much so that Violet half expected him to accidentally pull the trigger at any moment.

Preston must have thought so, too. His eyes met Violet's for a long moment, in which he seemed to be trying to telegraph something to her.

Or maybe ask permission for whatever he was about to try?

Violet moved her head in a barely perceptible nod. She might not trust Preston to share the credit on a case, but she trusted him not to get her killed.

Preston pointed over Blinder's shoulders to the porthole and yelled, "He's in here!"

If Blinder's nerves hadn't been worn so ragged, it would never have worked. But he had been hiding in the dark for hours, listening to naval officers search his ship, and probably wondering just how loyal to him his crew would be under questioning.

He jumped, looking reflexively behind him.

Preston moved so fast it was as though his joints were liquid. He sprang forward, wrenched the gun out of Blinder's hand, and used the butt of the weapon to hammer a vicious strike into the side of Blinder's head.

Blinder dropped like a stone, unconscious.

Violet released a breath. "Thank you."

"Don't mention it." Preston pocketed the gun and extended a hand towards the open space in the wall where Blinder had been hiding. "Want to see what else he's got in there?"

The sliding panel turned out to conceal a space about four feet wide and four feet deep, with the majority of the wall space being taken up by shelves.

Preston gave a low whistle at the sight of the bundles of notes—German marks—that were stacked up in neat rows on the shelves.

"Doesn't look like he's had the chance to spend much, if anything."

"And here's the receipt for the bonds." Violet had picked up a thick, official-looking envelope and revealed three sheets of thick, cream-coloured paper inside, each marked with the seal of the Berenberg Bank, Hamburg. She held it out to Preston.

He shook his head. "You keep it. Like I said before, that's a ticket to getting your job back at Pinkerton's."

"I don't think I want my old job back." Violet was even more surprised to hear those words come out of her mouth than Preston appeared to be.

Ever since that meeting in Mr. Pinkerton's office, she'd had a single goal: to prove to him once and for all what a colossal mistake he'd made in letting her go. But now, when the means to that end were literally right here in her grasp …

"I've discovered these past months that there's a great deal to be said for being out on your own: the ability to choose your own clients, pursue leads the way you see fit, answer to no one but yourself. Here. You take it."

Violet still couldn't entirely believe her own words, and yet the decision felt … right. Some deeply buried part of her had been working towards this moment for a long time, even without her consciously realising it.

She pushed the documents towards Preston again. "Mr. Pinkerton will probably pay you a bonus."

"Well, now." Preston looked down at the envelope between them and scratched his chin. "That could be a problem, since I've been thinking about resigning my position as one of his agents."

"You're leaving Pinkerton's?" Violet stared at him. "Why?"

"Everything you just said. I'd rather be independent, pick which cases I get to work on, handle things in the way that I want to. Once I get back to America, my plan is to hang out my shingle as a private detective." He stopped, seeming to hesitate for a moment, then looked at her. "Of course, if I was to do that, I'd rather have a partner in the business."

His gaze met Violet's. His usual slow, calm nonchalance had fallen away, and his blue eyes were watching her with focused intensity.

If she hadn't believed that the word could never apply to Preston, Violet would have said that he looked almost nervous. It mattered to him, whatever she was about to say next.

Violet said, slowly, "I've never had a partner before."

Preston searched her face, and seemed to read in her expression what she hadn't actually said out loud. He grinned.

"Well, as a very smart woman once said to me, there's a first time for everything."

Chapter 57: Watson

Sunday, October 28

I left our rooms on Baker Street just before noon, principally for a stroll but also to replenish my tobacco supply. There was a chill in the air as I returned. October was yielding to November, I remarked to myself. Soon winter would be upon us.

As I approached 221B I saw two black carriages at the curb in front of our home. I had a moment's trepidation. The Loch Ness adventure had begun with the kidnapping of Violet Leverton in a black carriage.

Then I saw that both the drivers and the footmen wore military uniforms, and the doors of both carriages were emblazoned with the seal of the Crown. Relief washed over me, followed by excitement. I had the vague inkling that medals might be in the offing.

I was wrong.

Mrs. Hudson met me at the door, her cheeks pink with excitement. "They've just gone upstairs," she said. "It's the Prime Minister himself. And Mr. Choate, the Ambassador from America."

I set my tobacco down on the hall bookshelf and mounted the seventeen steps with growing excitement. When I opened the door, both these official dignitaries were standing with Holmes in our sitting-room. Holmes wore his usual Sunday robe and battered slippers. The polished shoes and formal morning coats of our guests made a stark contrast. The Prime Minister's middle protruded like the prow of a ship beneath his grey silk waistcoat. His rotund face, so florid and vigorous when I had last seen him, now had a grey pallor. His beard, formerly black and curled luxuriantly like abundant sheep's wool, now was an old man's white and straggly affair. The election campaign had evidently taken its toll. Had he been my patient I should have recommended immediate rest.

The American Ambassador, a sad-faced greying man of perhaps sixty years, had a downturned mouth that suggested he had long since become resigned to the unhappy conditions of the world. His morning coat and striped trousers were of American cut, new and of finest quality. I had the fleeting suspicion that he had purchased them the previous year to be suitably attired for his new assignment.

"Ah, Dr. Watson, we were just becoming settled," Holmes said as I entered. He performed introductions, then directed the two men to the two corners of our settee. He took his customary chair alongside the glowing coals of our fireplace. I took my customary chair on the other side.

"Now, what can I do for you, gentlemen?" Holmes said.

The Prime Minister said, "First, we should like to offer our personal thanks and congratulations, as well as the formal gratitude of our respective governments. A catastrophe has been prevented. Suffering and death for thousands of innocent British citizens will not occur. Also, the election has concluded in our favour. It might have had a very different outcome, and for unjust reasons."

The Ambassador added, "My government is pleased that an American citizen has not succeeded in committing an attack of the vilest kind upon the citizens of our staunch ally. Besides which, our Treasury benefits by the return of stolen bonds of substantial value. All thanks to your acuity and swift action."

"Dr. Watson and I are naturally honoured to accept your thanks," Holmes said. In his armchair, he barely moved. His next words came softly, with that silken tone he takes on when he knows that he has the upper hand. "And now?"

The Prime Minister's tone grew more sombre. "Now, Mr. Holmes, we come to you concerned with justice and retribution."

Holmes nodded. "But surely such matters are the province of the British justice system. Blinder and his henchman are both in the hands of the law, and the evidence should be sufficient to convict and hang them both. They are co-conspirators in the murder of the three Campbells, and in the murder of the messenger who delivered the stolen bonds from the Junior Carlton Club, as well as the death of the innocent janitor at St. Thomas Hospital. To say nothing of the attempts at mass murder that did not succeed."

"They will plead not guilty," said the PM.

"But they will be convicted in the end. The weight of evidence is on the side of the Crown."

"That may very well be. But bringing that evidence to the jury will mean bringing it to the public."

"I expected as much. You wish to keep the matter from the public."

"It would inevitably come out that the Germans had been involved. We expect Blinder to claim that he was the unwitting dupe of the Kaiser. The result would be public rage and an immediate outcry for war. And Her Majesty's Government has quite enough war to contend with at the moment, both in South Africa and in China."

I stared, aghast. The room seemed to sway around me. "Surely Blinder and Romain are not to escape justice?" I could not accept that outcome. Not after all our trials and endangerments. I glanced at Holmes, who sat, serene and dispassionate. My emotions must have shown, for he raised a forefinger a fraction of an inch, pointing in my direction.

Then Holmes said, "I take it our American friends would also prefer to avoid a trial?"

The Ambassador nodded. "This is an election year for us as well. Voting in the United States will be held eight days from now, on Tuesday next. Blinder was a substantial contributor to Mr. McKinley's first campaign. A grave embarrassment, to say the least, if our opponents were to learn of his treachery."

Holmes turned up a palm. "You are not suggesting, however, that either of your governments lacks the fortitude to proceed with a trial if there is no other alternative?"

"Certainly not. We come to you, however, in the hope that you can suggest a way to achieve justice without the public disruption that a trial would cause."

For a long moment Holmes sat silent, his hands clasped, his fingertips steepled. Then he said, "Before I can recommend a solution, I need some additional facts."

"Name them," the Ambassador said.

"Where are the bonds?"

"In the US Treasury office in Washington. They were sent by the Berenberg Bank through the usual official banking channels, with the formal application for their redemption."

"Has the Treasury complied?"

"Not as yet."

Holmes nodded. "Where is the cash—the German marks?"

"In the hands of the Treasury as well. Delivered, with the receipt documents, by the former Pinkerton agents Mr. Preston and Miss Leverton."

"In Washington?"

"Yes."

"How much cash would the marks fetch in dollars?"

"$$1.5 million at today's exchange rate."

"For three million in bearer bonds?"

"The marks were an advance on the full value. The German bank agreed to provide the remainder to Blinder when the US Treasury had made full redemption. Those terms are set forth in the receipt documents."

"So, from a financial standpoint, the Treasury has benefited, at least temporarily, by $$4.5 million. It has not yet paid out three million dollars to redeem the bonds, and in addition has in its possession $$1.5 million in cash—albeit in German marks."

"Quite so," the Ambassador replied. "By the way, I understand that the Treasury has made a generous reward to Pinkerton's for the successful completion of the assignment. A bonus well above and beyond the fee agreed upon."

Holmes appeared not to notice. He asked, "Where are Blinder and Romain?"

"In the brig of HMS *Daring*, here in Victoria Docks."

"Have you seen either of them?"

"No. They have repeatedly asked my embassy to intervene, but as yet I have declined."

"Where is the *Avenger*?"

"Also in Victoria Docks. Confiscated by Her Majesty's Navy."

"And the crew?"

"They were deported back to America. After giving affidavits that incriminated Blinder and Romain."

"I take it the crew exonerated themselves with their testimony?" I asked.

"As one would expect."

"And where is the submarine they used to lend credence to the rumours of a monster in Loch Ness?" Holmes asked.

"On board the *Avenger*," said the Prime Minister. "Though we have agreed to turn the submarine over to the American Navy when it is no longer needed as evidence."

"The plans are American and were stolen," said the Ambassador. "Under American law, the vessel belongs to the Navy."

Holmes gave one of his disinterested shrugs. "And the poison stored in the submarine?"

The PM's mouth turned down in distaste. "Incinerated."

"That is just as well." Holmes said.

He leaned forward, his grey eyes bright. "I do have a recommendation. It is not without risk. You will both need to cooperate promptly and fully."

Both our guests were old and practiced negotiators. The PM gave the barest of nods. The American asked, "What did you have in mind?"

"You, Mr. Ambassador, will direct the US Treasury to cable the Berenberg Bank in Hamburg, giving notice that no redemption of the bonds will be made."

"On what grounds?"

"That the bonds appear to be forgeries."

"But the bonds are genuine. Stolen, but quite genuine nonetheless."

"Doubtless the Berenberg Bank will send a return cable disputing the decision. You will ask to be informed as soon as that happens."

"I see. What else, Mr. Holmes?"

"When the return cable has arrived, you will advise your counterpart, the German Ambassador, that you are requesting Her Majesty's government to deport Mr. Blinder and Mr. Romain to Germany."

Both our guests drew in their breaths.

The Prime Minister said, "So the Germans will believe they have been swindled. When those two criminals arrive, the reception will be a hot one. The Germans will demand the return of 1.5 million dollars' worth of German Marks."

"And when payment is not forthcoming," said the Ambassador, "presumably the Germans will exact revenge."

* * *

The plan worked. Blinder and Romain, unaware that the United States Treasury had refused payment on the stolen bonds, entered Germany willingly. They were taken into custody by German police at the port of Hamburg.

Their bodies were found floating in the harbour two days later.

Chapter 58: Becky

December 15, 1900

The envelope was addressed to her, Rebecca Kelly, in care of Mr. Sherlock Holmes, 221B Baker Street, London. She took care to observe it first, noting the thick crème-coloured paper, the exquisitely penned letters of the address, and the gilt-edged monogram on the back. The text beneath the monogram indicated that the letter came from the Trust Department of the J.P Morgan Bank, 60 Victoria Embankment, London.

"There is an identical missive for Flynn as well," Mr. Holmes said. "I shall see that he gets it whenever he arrives."

"They both came in today's mail," said Dr. Watson.

Becky opened it carefully. She saw the same gilt-edged monogram atop a single sheet of heavy crème-coloured paper.

She read:

> *Dear Miss Kelly:*
>
> *This will serve notice that a trust fund has been established in your name at the J. P. Morgan Bank, by Trustors Miss Violet Leverton and Mr. Beauregard Preston, of New York City in the United States of America. The initial corpus of ten thousand pounds sterling will be invested on your behalf. The funds and any earnings thereon will be made available to*

you for educational purposes at any time. Upon your attaining the age of twenty-five years, the funds and any earnings thereon will be available for any purpose that you may elect.

Please call upon me at your convenience.

Your obedient servant,
J. Whitmore Wilcox, Trustee

P.S.: Miss Leverton and Mr. Preston wish you to know that they both still consider themselves to be in your debt.

THE END

Historical Note

This is a work of fiction, and the authors make no claim whatsoever that any historical locations or historical figures who appear in this story were even remotely connected with the adventures and events recounted herein.

However …

1. The 1900 United Kingdom general election was known as "the Khaki Election," since khaki was the colour of uniforms worn by the British soldiers and a principal issue of the campaign at the time was public expenditure on the war being conducted in South Africa. Opponents of the war did make an issue of purportedly neglected maintenance of public infrastructure, to underscore what they believed was improper use of public funds on empire-building by Prime Minister Salisbury and the Conservative Party.

2. The election was a close one. The Conservative Party lost nine seats in Parliament but maintained power with 50.2 per cent of the popular vote.

3. In November 1900, Lord Salisbury resigned from his position as Foreign Secretary, but maintained his position of Prime Minister. He resigned as Prime Minister in July of 1902, due to his ill health, and died the following year.

4. The 1900 programme of the Highland Games did include a 100-yard egg-and-spoon race for young girls ages 14 and under.

5. At the time of this adventure Urquhart Castle was a somewhat disreputable ruin languishing in private ownership. In 1913 the castle was taken over by the state and partially restored. Today the castle is one of the most popular tourist attractions in Scotland. It was also used as a setting for the 1970 film, *The Private Life of Sherlock Holmes*.

6. The authors have found no historical reference to any actual attempts to poison the London water supply in 1900. However, ricin has been employed for politically motivated purposes in London as recently as 1978, when a ricin pellet was injected under the skin of a Bulgarian journalist by means of an umbrella, the tip of which had been modified for the purpose. The journalist died four days later.

Lucy James will return.

A Note of Thanks

Thank you for reading *The Loch Ness Horror*. We hope you've enjoyed it.

As you probably know, reviews make a big difference! So, we also hope you'll consider going back to the Amazon page where you bought the story and uploading a quick review. You can get to that page by going to this link on our website and scrolling down:

sherlockandlucy.com/project/the-loch-ness-horror/

You can also sign up for our mailing list at
www.SherlockandLucy.com
and get a FREE download of four adventures and audiobooks

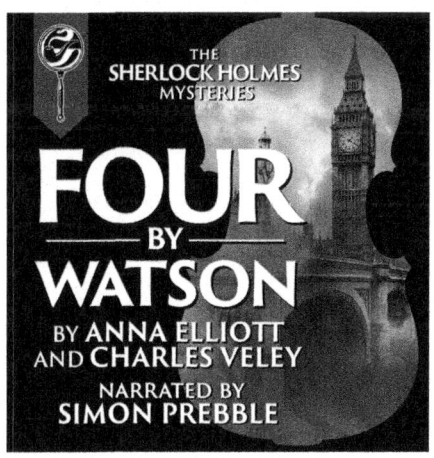

About the Authors

Anna Elliott is the author of the *Twilight of Avalon* trilogy, and *The Pride and Prejudice Chronicles*. She was delighted to lend a hand in giving the character of Lucy James her own voice, firstly because she loves Sherlock Holmes as much as her father, Charles Veley, and second because it almost never happens that someone with a dilemma shouts, "Quick, we need an author of historical fiction!" She lives in Pennsylvania with her husband and five children.

Charles Veley is the author of the first two books in this series of fresh Sherlock Holmes adventures. He is thrilled to be contributing Dr. Watson's chapters for the series, and delighted beyond words to be collaborating with Anna Elliott.

Printed in Great Britain
by Amazon